A Soldier's Crest

The Dragon Knight Chronicles

To Ruben,
Thank you for the support!
Best Wishes,
Joseph Angotti

JOSEPH ANGOTTI

THE POLYETHNIC PUBLISHING
UNITED STATES OF AMERICA

Invictus, is an imprint of The Polyethnic Publishing, LLC.

A Soldier's Crest: The Dragon Knight Chronicles

The Polyethnic Publishing, LLC
e-mail: contact@thepolyethnic.com
www.thepolyethnic.com

Printed in the United States of America

First Paperback Edition, July 2017
Cover Illustration © 2017 by Gabriella Dennany
Formatted by Melissa M. Futrell

ISBN-13: 978-1-946105-18-9
ISBN-10: 1-946105-18-X

In Loving Memory of
Andrew Enderud

Prologue

"Let's go, Dawn!" Faris held Dawn by the hand as they scurried through the Davish Forest. It was easily the most dangerous area for children to play in, but Dawn and Faris spent most of their afternoons exploring it. Vines and branches danced in the wind generated by their running.

"Mom is going to kill us!" yelled Dawn, hoping that Faris would hear her over all the noise they were making. She used her free hand to hold the flower that she had plucked from the forest and placed in her dark black hair.

Faris was faster than Dawn, but Dawn was much more agile. Faris bolted through the forest with Dawn, calling out each branch to dodge along the way. When the two children emerged from the forest, they were on the other side of town. The field they ran on was a sea of tall green grass that the sun, now piercing the morning sky, reflected its honey-like rays upon. In the distance there were farms that appeared as specks on the landscape and in the middle of the plains was a large mansion, its hickory wood walls made lighter in the brightness of the day.

As Dawn and Faris made their way through the field at a hurried pace, they couldn't help but stop to admire the fruit growing on the bushes as they passed them. Faris pointed at a particular juicy-looking Arrett, a fruit that resembled an apple. Faris plucked it from the bush and much to Dawn's disapproval, took a bite out of it. He then tossed the Arrett to Dawn, before he continued running in the direction of the mansion. She shook her head, laughed and snuck in a bite of her own before discarding the fruit on the ground.

Faris won the race back to the mansion, as he often did. He took a round key out of his pocket and opened the front door.

"Wait! Shoes off," Dawn said. "You know how my parents are."

"I thought all of the mud fell off with how fast I was going," Faris said with a smile, unaware of the dirt on his forehead, just below his brown hair. "I think you have dust on your shirt."

"Ha, ha... You're so funny." Dawn kicked off her shoes that were definitely not made for running through a forest, and then stepped past Faris into the house.

"Mom! We're home!" she made her way into the dining room. Her mother was sitting at the table with a large book in front of her. The woman was as beautiful as she was wise, and age did not seem to stunt either.

Her long flowing black hair matched her daughter's, and the hardly visible wrinkles beginning to form on her face only complimented her beauty instead of diminishing it.

"Playing in the forest again, I see." Dawn's mother pulled out the chair beside her so that Dawn could sit.

"Hello, Mrs. Wyndar," Faris said with a smile as he entered the room. He wasn't nearly as dirty as Dawn, despite having led the way back. Dawn wondered how he pulled that off. Maybe it did fall off while he was running so fast.

"Hello Faris," Mrs. Wyndar pulled out the chair on the opposite side of Dawn for him.

"What are we learning today?" Faris asked, hopping up onto the chair. "Are we picking up from where we left off yesterday?"

Mrs. Wyndar patted the book in front of her. "Not quite," she said simply. "I had Nikolai go out and pick up this book from the Earth Mother yesterday."

Dawn's eyes lit up. "A book directly from the Earth Mother?" The Earth Mother was a mysterious being, living in a secluded forest said to be protected by angels. Her wisdom was unmatched, and her knowledge of the old world was vast. "Does it explain what the world was like before?"

"Before...?" Mrs. Wyndar looked at Dawn, then at Faris. "Do you recall the lesson from a few days ago? What was the cataclysmic event that is responsible for our world?"

"I forgot," said Dawn. "We spoke about it last week."

“The Streeges,” Faris said promptly.

“Close, Faris,” Mrs. Wyndar smiled. “It’s called ‘The Strages’. An overwhelming event that left our world in shambles. Had it not been for the angels from Heaven, this world would have ended and we wouldn’t be sitting here today.”

Dawn leaned forward looking at the cover of the book. “Does this book talk about the Strages?”

“Even better, my dear.” As Mrs. Wyndar opened the book with a creak, Dawn noticed some dust coming off the book. The pages were yellow and most of the writing looked faded. “This book is a record of the life and the world before the Strages. What people were like, what they went through, the places they lived and traveled. It also touches down on the events that led to the Strages and the people involved.”

Faris was also leaning forward in his chair in interest. “This is the history of our world?” he exclaimed. “That is so cool!”

“Indeed,” Mrs. Wyndar said as she flipped to the next page. A drawing on the right depicted a large skyscraper. “Though we’re fortunate to live in one of the largest buildings on Khroma, buildings in the old world towered over this one. Similar to the lighthouse not too far from here, but even bigger than that.”

“They lived in giant towers?” Dawn asked. “How did they climb them?”

“Stairs similar to the ones we use were used back then, but they also had these square devices that transported you from the bottom to whatever floor you wanted.”

“Did they have a name?” asked Faris.

"Elevators."

Before Mrs. Wyndar could continue, a large man with a light grey beard and grey hair walked into the room. The three at the table turned their attention to him immediately. His large presence commanded the attention of the room.

"Hello, Dawn. Hello, Faris." The large man spoke, his booming voice filling the room.

"Hello, father," Dawn replied with a smile.

"Hello, Mr. Wyndar," added Faris.

"Aurora, may I have a word?" The man asked, and left the room before receiving Mrs. Wyndar's reply.

"Read through the book, and ask me any questions you have when I return. Please just take care of the book. It's old and I must return it to the Earth Mother tomorrow." Aurora brought her index finger and thumb up to Dawn's chin, before sliding her chair out and leaving the table. The two children immediately pounced on the book.

"What's wrong, Edgar?" Aurora walked past her husband and opened a cabinet, removing a tall glass from it and placing it down on the counter in front of her.

"Aurora, I know you want to teach the children about the past but I believe it's time we teach them what they need to survive in this world," Edgar replied.

Aurora poured herself a glass of water. "Are we really cutting into the children's education to have this conversation again?" she said. "Dawn will inherit the family business, and it's important that she is well-educated so that she may carry herself properly throughout Khroma."

"And Faris? Will the upper class of Khroma really respect a woman who travels with a poor boy?" Edgar asked, following suit with his wife and poured himself a glass of water. "We can only cover up the fact that he is from an orphanage for so long. People will question where he comes from and he's obviously not one of ours."

"We'll worry about that when the time comes. It will be easier to explain to Faris when they're older that he needs to simply be her bodyguard and nothing more," Aurora explained.

"Dawn wouldn't need a bodyguard if we allowed her to get proper training. If we teach her how to fight at an early age, she would be able to protect herself. Your very own teachings demonstrate how this world is in disarray. It's not the easiest place to grow up wealthy. Everyone sees a target on our backs. They all want a piece of our money and success, and some will stop at nothing to take everything we own. There will come a time when Faris isn't enough to protect her, and she'll need to stand on her own."

Aurora put her glass down on the table and fixated her eyes on her husband. "We agreed to bring only one child into this world. Dawn is that child. Dawn is the only one that can carry on our legacy. I will not raise her like some barbarian from Tark," she argued. "She will be elegant and presentable, a woman worthy of the fortune we will pass onto her. Her knowledge will rival that of the Earth Mother's when I'm done with her."

Edgar put his glass down on the table, removed one of the chairs and sat down. He hung his head, as if admitting defeat to his wife. "I still think we're making a mistake sending her out into this world without preparing her for it. There are monsters, dragons and demons out there. What may be the worst of them all, are the people who will try to do her harm."

Aurora walked over and put her arm around her husband's shoulders. "I understand your concern, honey, but Dawn will not become one of these savages. She deserves to be placed on a pedestal, like the Earth Mother before her."

"I think I should decide." The tiny voice came from the entrance of the room.

"Dawn, how long were you listening?" asked Aurora, taken aback.

"Long enough." Faris entered the room behind her as she spoke. "I don't want to spend my whole life here, running the business. I want to go out and explore, like how Faris and I explore the Davish Forest. I want to make a difference in this world that isn't just from staying here in our mansion, while Nikolai and others run errands for me. I don't want Faris to be my bodyguard, he is my friend. I want to be able to take up arms beside him and strike down whatever is threatening us."

"We have a long time before we need to make any decisions, Dawn." Edgar intervened, though her interest in being strong enough to defend herself made him smile.

"Not that long, father. Time passes quickly and soon I will need to know how to fight."

Chapter One

The bells of the Bawal Empire's throne room rang loudly as the army gathered. King Rebel stood in front of his throne, dressed in all black as he usually was. A few servants came over to him and checked if he needed anything. Standing in front of him was a large man, also dressed in black, wearing a cape with a gold dragon on it. In one hand, was a helmet with some dents in it and in the other, was a large dragon's tooth. The tooth was large enough to cover the length of the man's fingers to his forearm, and was yellow with a hint of green at the root. He was having a difficult time holding it. The King motioned to one of the servants. Hastily, they left and soon returned with a chalice of wine.

"That will be all," said the King, and the servants went back to their places besides the elevated platform where the King's throne and his most trusted knights and comrades stood. As the King took his seat on the throne, the people in the crowd began to talk amongst themselves. Most of the people invited to this hearing were talking about the mysterious man in the cape with the dragon's tooth.

One whispered to the other, "No last name, no hometown. Does no one know anything about this guy?"

"They call him 'Griffen' and he is a very skilled fighter. That's about all we know," his friend replied.

"As skilled as the mighty Synthro?" someone behind them chimed in.

"Doubtful," another in the crowd responded. "Synthro would've dragged the entire dragon in here, not just a tooth," he continued.

Another man felt it necessary to put in his two cents. "Synthro isn't real, quit believin' the rumors. No one has seen the guy!"

The first man who spoke laughed. "My friend here just told me that until a few days ago, no one had seen this Griffen fellow either," he finished, and suddenly everyone grew silent. A horn sounded and King Rebel rose to speak.

Griffen put his head back for a moment and reflected on what led to this meeting. Two days ago, Griffen had heard rumors of a menace troubling the people of a town called Davish. This town was located just outside Sanctiveil, a kingdom located in the northern region of the main continent known as Khroma. When Griffen arrived, the people of the town spoke of a wicked dragon terrorizing them.

"Bax, the terror of Davish," one villager said.

Griffen was seated in a pub, listening to the cries of the people. "Bax?" he asked, taking a drink.

"That's the name of the dragon," the man replied.

Griffen stared at the man, as if he had something on his face. "The name of the dragon? Did he peek his head out and tell you his name?"

The villager thought about his statement for a moment, but Griffen placed his drink down and stood up, interrupting his thoughts. "What else do you know of this dragon?"

"Everyone who goes into his cave is burned alive or eaten, or burned and then eaten. We don't know much else," another villager explained.

"That isn't much help," Griffen said, walking out of the pub, some of the desperate villagers following him. "The cave is east?"

"Yes, just before Pura," one of the villagers replied. Pura was a town belonging to Sanctiveil.

Griffen did not say another word. He adjusted the belt attached to the sheath of his sword, and adjusted his cape as well to prevent the rope keeping it on his back from bothering his neck. He walked out of the village in the direction of the cave.

"He's going alone? He knows it's a high dragon, right?"

"Another will fall to Bax."

By the time Griffen reached the cave, the day had surrendered to night and Griffen was forced to light a torch before entering.

Maybe I should wait till morning, he thought. The shadows moved around him as if to sway him to proceed further. He walked quietly as he moved the torch to expose his surroundings. All he found were bones of those who came before him. After a few moments of slow footsteps, he heard the loud breathing of the beast. He raised his torch to reveal the high dragon, known to the villagers as Bax. Known to him as something else entirely.

The dragon was enormous. Griffen wondered how it fit inside the cave to begin with, and knew its lack of movement would be to his benefit. It was sitting up against the wall, its long neck curved against the cave's ceiling, its tiny hands full of sharp claws placed on its bulging belly – no doubt filled with those who came before Griffen in an effort to thwart the threat of the dragon. Its face was long and consisted almost entirely of its jaw and long sharp teeth. Tiny eyes protruded from its skull and two small holes formed the nostrils that were pushing smoke out every time the beast snored. A bit of drool and remnants of blood dripped from its mouth.

"Avernax. One of the first high dragons ever born," Griffen shouted, stirring the beast from its slumber.

Avernax leaned forward, startled and angry. Its quick reaction forced flames out from its mouth, which Griffen quickly evaded. He placed himself behind a rock to avoid any further attacks and grabbed the handle of his blade without removing it from its sheath just yet.

"I did not expect you to move to a home so far removed from the Faux," Griffen laughed, but the dragon advanced to his right, forcing him to move around the rock. "Skye must not be happy with your departure."

"Speak your name, human. How do you come upon mine?"

"Ah, yes," Griffen commented, as he revealed himself from behind the rock. "One of the few high dragons whose tongue can form words."

"I have never seen you before, yet your knowledge of Dragonkin is vast. Who are you, human?"

"Do not ask again," Griffen said as drew his sword. When he looked up, he noticed that Avernax's wings did not even fit inside the cave, they were pinned to the walls. "Not the wisest of homes for a dragon as large as yourself."

Avernax blew more fire and Griffen once again found refuge behind the rock. The fire that lingered on the ground provided extra light as Griffen watched the shadows on the wall dance.

"As if you would know, human. You are but a speck on the ground to me," Avernax gritted.

Griffen laughed. "Your flames do not scare me, Avernax."

Griffen expected an answer, but the answer took a more violent form than he anticipated. Avernax jumped forward and swiped his claw, demolishing the rock that Griffen hid behind. "It was foolish to come alone, human."

Avernax brought his mouth down with a bite, but Griffen parried the attack with his sword and jumped backwards to keep space between them. The dragon advanced and blew more fire in his direction but the shadows on the wall, created by the fire, gathered in front of Griffen and formed a wall that blocked the attack and dissipated the flames around him.

"The darkness fights for you?"

"And for that reason, I am never alone," Griffen said as his sword flew through the shadow wall and found the skin just under the dragon's mouth, one of the few soft spots on a dragon's body. The dragon roared and leaned back, but the shadows formed ropes that pinned the beast to the ground. Blood streamed from its wound and splashed the ground when Griffen removed his blade. "Let all of those who brought the fall of my true kin, find justice in the form of my blade, and regret the mistake of leaving one member of the Frostfear tribe alive!"

The dragon's eyes grew wide. "His child...? Impossible!"

Griffen brought his sword up and brought it down to rip the dragon's throat apart.

***

"Let us pay tribute to the savior of Davish!" King Rebel's words brought Griffen back to the present. "And ask, what the mighty Griffen wants as his reward?"

"I wish only to serve Khroma and remove any other dragons that pose a threat to our beloved continent," Griffen replied simply.

"You suggest we start a war with the dragons? Skye Highborn has shown no interest in feuding with our kind."

Their words caused a stir in the crowd behind

them.

"It is only a matter of time before the Dragonkin become like Bax, turning their flames upon us. It is simple fact that creatures that deem themselves superior to other creatures feel the need to conquer those they feel are weaker." Griffen spoke grimly as he turned to the crowd. "Will we stand idly by, as the Dragonkin amass a force that humans cannot possibly compete with? Surely you have all seen the high dragons soar the skies above the Dragon Faux."

"Their flames will destroy our cities!" one man cried out.

"Our homes and fields!" another answered.

"Do you wish for your people to live in fear, until the dragons destroy us? Or will you rise above the threat and crush it before we are devoured?" Griffen asked, his voice echoing through the room.

"What do you suggest?" asked the King.

The feeble minds of Bawal are easy to manipulate, Griffen thought.

"Give me an army and I will march into the Dragon Faux and outsmart the Dragonkin and see that they fall," he spoke aloud.

"An entire army? No." The King replied firmly, and the crowd erupted in protest. "I will not forfeit my entire army to be slaughtered by dragons while Sanctiveil and Azuldra pose a threat. We will be too vulnerable."

"I need men to fight the dragons," Griffen said. "Defeating one alone was no easy task, I cannot defeat them all alone."

"I will give you resources to recruit your own men.

Find the strongest among us and get them to support you, and perhaps I will lend you my support," King Rebel sat back down in his chair. The people of his empire were furious and yelling behind Griffen. "Shadow, come here."

A figure emerged from the darkness behind the throne holding a large book under his arm. His entire body was covered in a black cloak and the darkness covered all but the bottom of his face.

"I knew you would ask for this book, my Lord. Here it is," Shadow said as he held the book out to the king.

"Do not hand it to me, you useless wretch. I would not touch such a decrepit thing. Give it to the Dragon Slayer."

Shadow walked over to Griffen and handed him the book.

Griffen was confused by the gesture. "Forgive me, Your Majesty. What does this book contain?"

"A list. Mostly made up of places that don't even exist anymore," King Rebel laughed. "Amidst the text you may find a place or two of use in finding your men."

"I killed a high dragon by myself and you present me a book of outdated information?"

"I present you opportunity. Form a group of knights under my rule and I will double your numbers. Then you can have your war with the dragons."

Griffen went to speak, but the King stood again and cut him off. "That is enough for the day."

The King left the room with Shadow and his knights behind him. Still angry, the townspeople were talking loudly as they began to leave as well. Griffen clutched the book tightly and exited the room.

A tall knight in black armor stopped Griffen with his hand as he was walking out. "I would have words, Dragon Slayer," he said. The knight was holding a black helmet with two points sticking out on either side. Around his waist was a one handed mace, which Griffen found odd as most knights of Bawal were known for wielding swords...all but one.

"General Gerard Pace," said Griffen. "I expected you to be standing behind your King's throne, where most generals reside during meetings."

"You know of me?"

"I make note of all of the generals of Khroma. Max Alexian of Sanctiveil, Khelban Ace Syden of Azuldra and Alencia Skyfall of Ruebrum."

"Many do not know I own the title for Bawal," Gerard said, walking out towards a training area set up just outside the castle walls. Griffen followed suit.

"A title seemingly wasted in a Kingdom such as this," Griffen huffed. Gerard stopped to stare at him. "Forgive my rudeness. King Rebel's words have..."

Gerard shook his head. "Do not apologize. You are right. For years I have served as General of Bawal, yet no one even knows. There is no honor in being the general in an army uninterested in progress. We sit by, idly, waiting for an attack from Azuldra or Ruebrum. We sit around waiting for Max Alexian to lead Sanctiveil into Bawal for revenge, yet it has been years since Bawal marched on them and there has been no signs of retaliation."

"Then what do you spend your days doing?"

"Watching over the new recruits as they train. I provide helpful tips on how to be a warrior, but there are no warriors here, I'm afraid. The men the King sends me to train are not fit to wield a sword, nor do they have the mind for it."

"Think of the glory that would be bestowed upon you if you were to bring down the mighty dragons located in the Faux," Griffen insisted. "At least that's what I think to myself."

"You might be onto something," Gerard said. "Something I may want to be a part of, something more interesting than this."

"You are the General of Bawal, I would not take you away from that."

"Come, Dragon Slayer," Gerard motioned Griffen over with his hand. "I want to show you something."

Gerard led Griffen out to where a few knights were being trained. Some were using swords with shields, a few wielded maces like the general and some had two-handed swords. Majority of these men were clumsy with their attacks, leaving openings that Griffen noted in his mind, before the general interrupted his thoughts.

"You can see more clearly now that there are no soldiers among them. This is what King Rebel has us do, day in and day out, but it is all for naught."

"Forgive me if I'm overstepping my boundaries, General, but perhaps the fault lies in the men training these boys," suggested Griffen.

"A keen observation, which I will get back to. The mage who brought you the book with the information," Gerard paused and interrupted one boy's training to correct his stance.

"I believe he is called Shadow," said Griffen as

Gerard joined him.

"Yes, he is no ordinary mage. The man is a necromancer, a specialist when it comes to resurrecting the dead."

Griffen looked around him. "He intends for these boys to die for his experiments?" he asked in surprise. "There are hundreds of boys here."

"Boys that will have their skeletons reanimated to fight Rebel's wars for him."

"And what of you, General?"

"He will keep his real warriors alive, to keep order within his ranks. To have soldiers to send to the other armies for the sake of conversation," Gerard stopped in front of the final group of boys training. Unlike the others, these boys were all in proper formation and swinging their weapons like real warriors. "There is no honor in leading a bunch of lifeless skeletons. I am ashamed to be the general of this empire. I will not become just a simple messenger when I stand his greatest warrior."

"One I had the honor of molding," a deep voice joined their quiet conversation. A wide man stood in front of the boys training, both of his hands behind his back. His gray hair was spiked on one side, flattened in the middle and then spiked again on the other. On his back was a large round shield and sheathed on his waist was a long silver blade with a black handle.

Gerard gestured to him. "This is what I wanted to show you, Dragon Slayer. The only group of boys that won't die and become skeletons. They have been trained by a dear friend of mine, Wyglaf Flace."

"It is an honor to meet you, Wyglaf," Griffen

offered his hand as Wyglaf turned around.

"Likewise," Wyglaf accepted the gesture. "I hear you defeated the dragon near Davish. You will have to tell me about how you did it so that I can teach my men."

"You will not be teaching these men for much longer, I'm afraid," added Gerard.

"What do you mean, General?" Wyglaf stood tall in respect to Gerard.

"How do you consider your ability to judge a man's true worth?"

"A man's true worth is hard to judge, General, but when it comes to a man's fighting ability, I stand unequaled." Wyglaf placed his right hand on the handle of his blade. "I can see the true potential in men and if they will amount to anything on the battlefield."

"Your art?" asked Griffen.

"Just a gift, Dragon Slayer. Born from experience," answered Wyglaf.

"Then if Griffen and I were to travel the world in search of the strongest warriors in Khroma, your gift would be rather helpful." Gerard spoke earnestly.

Wyglaf rubbed the gray beard on his face. "Gather the strongest fighters in the world? To what end?"

"The General is interested in helping me rid the world of the Dragonkin," said Griffen.

"I'm too old to be running around fighting dragons," Wyglaf said through a muffled laugh.

"Age was never an excuse for you before, Wyglaf. Your talents are wasted here. You train men to die, nothing more. Soon our army will be nothing but bones," Gerard spoke too loudly and some of the men stopped their training.

"Prove the General wrong, boys. Carry on!" shouted Wyglaf before joining Gerard and Griffen farther from the troops. "Have you found out more about the King and Shadow's plans that I don't know about?"

"He has successfully made a few skeletons, he just needs the corpses to make more. These men are intended to be those corpses."

"And what of us?" Wyglaf asked.

"He told me that I would continue to serve, to act as a messenger to other armies and nothing more. He made no mention of you," Gerard shook his head. "I will not sit by idly as our King makes a mockery of our army, casting aside all of our efforts so that he can win his wars with forbidden magic."

Wyglaf glanced between the two men with uncertainty. "Our only hope to fight honorably is to fight the dragons then? Has the King agreed to let you do this?"

"Not yet, but the King has given Griffen permission to form his own group of Dragon Knights. If we both join him then our lives will not be forfeited for some necromancer's schemes."

"But the lives of these men..." Wyglaf trailed off. He turned his attention back to the boys he was training.

"Lost whether you're here or not, I'm afraid," added Griffen, who had held his silence until then. "Traveling with me in search of the strongest warriors on Khroma will guarantee your life is not among the ones lost for this cause."

"Then let us go," said Wyglaf. "I will not be

associated with this madness."

"We will need enough supplies to travel north to Azuldra. That should be our first stop. Sanctiveil and Ruebrum require us to cross past Davish into Dragonkin territory," explained Griffen.

"That would be the smartest approach," agreed Wyglaf. "The mages of Azuldra are the best on Khroma, and it would be wise to get one into our group."

"Preferably one that specializes in water or ice magic," added Griffen.

"I know of one," Gerard said. "We will see if he still calls Azuldra his home when we get there. I will have some servants prepare supplies and some horses for us. How soon should we leave?"

"As soon as possible," said Griffen. "Let us not waste more time here in Bawal. With you two accompanying me, I can't envision stronger or better candidates."

"I will help make preparations," Wyglaf said heading in the direction of the stables.

"Allow me to join you so that I may better gauge what our supplies look like," Griffen added, following alongside Wyglaf.

"I will join the both of you shortly. There are some matters I must attend to before I leave," Gerard said and walked away in the opposite direction.

***

Gerard rode a horse east of his King's castle, the Corpus Castle. He entered into the village of Diremoore, his horse doing its best to avoid the cracks and crevices that made up its ground. Towards the back of the village, stood a large building with multiple sets of stairs leading to a door. A sign just outside the gate leading to the stairs read: “Pace Manor.”

Gerard pulled his horse past the sign and through the opening of the gate, tying it to the fence. He stared up at the house he grew up in. Memories of the good old days passed through his mind, but then he recalled the last time he had been home.

The entire village of Diremoore could be seen from the third floor balcony of the Pace house. Every single crack in the land, every disfigured tree, and even the disgruntled citizens traversing the dirt-filled walkways. Gerard, the oldest of four children, stood on the balcony. His charcoal black armor covered him from the neck down, his trademark horned helmet was tucked tightly under his arm and a long black cape with the skeleton head sigil of the Bawal Empire was on his back. The Corpus Castle of the Bawal Empire was also visible from the balcony, and gathered the majority of Gerard’s attention.

“How long do you plan on staring out that window?” said a soft voice from behind him.

“How long have you been standing there, Amily?” Gerard did not turn to meet her gaze.

“Long enough to realize that the man standing before me is no longer my brother,” she answered.

“I will always be your brother,” Gerard turned around to face her, Corpus Castle standing tall in the distance behind him. “A title won’t change that.”

“You are the General of Bawal now. You will never have time to visit us,” she said and looked away

from him, trying to hide how sad she was. She wanted to be happy for her brother. "Ever since father passed, you have kept this family afloat."

He pushed the strands of her long brown hair that covered her face out of the way. "I became General of Bawal to continue to do so. It is the only reason I do what I do. You're aware of that, aren't you?"

"Father would be so proud of you," she finally said in reply.

"I am honored to continue his legacy."

"He was a knight too, yes, but not a general! He is remembered by us and his closest companions - you will go down as a legend!" She finally let loose a smile as she spoke.

"A legend? You really think so?" Gerard returned the smile. "I think you're getting a bit ahead of yourself."

"King Rebel hardly uses his Knights, but now that he has named a General, he has to use you!"

Gerard was snapped back to the present by the creaking of the front door of his house. The fact that it was unlocked worried him.

He made his way up the long sets of stairs and pushed his way inside. "Amily?" he called out. "Your brother is home!"

A tall woman with long brown hair emerged from one of the rooms of the house. "Gerard, is that you? I almost didn't recognize you without your helmet on," she said with a smile.

"Very funny," Gerard embraced her with a hug. "You look skinny."

"Thank you, brother!" she exclaimed. She smiled as she made her way back into the room she emerged from. Gerard followed her.

"I didn't mean that as a compliment. Have you been eating? I've been sending money whenever I am able." The room Gerard followed her into was a kitchen, but most of the cabinets were bare, the sink had only a few dishes in it and the dining table had nothing on it.

"Mom is sick again," Amily said, reaching into one of the cabinets and pulling out a glass before sticking her hand in for another. "I've had to pay the healers here to help her get medicine and find some comfort, but the money isn't enough. I've tried to do some local work myself, but I'm just not strong enough to help with what needs to be done here."

"I can put in a word at the pub, you can be a waitress again."

She poured them both water and put Gerard's glass on the table and slid it towards him.

"Don't you think I've already tried that? They won't take me back. They say I scare too many people off."

"You scare people off? The hell does that mean?"

"You see the way Rebel treats his people. If they hire me, our customers will think that any form of disrespect would incur punishment from the hands of Rebel. After all, I'm the sister of the great Bawal General." She took a sip of her water.

"That's ridiculous. They won't hire you because of me?"

"That's the gist of it, yeah." She leaned her back against the sink and put her head back. "We're in a bad way here, Gerard."

"I'll go talk to them." He finished his water and put it down on the table.

"I think you're missing the point. You going to talk to them is exactly why they won't hire me in the first place."

Gerard stopped and look at her, and the way he looked at her crushed her. Here was her brother, the General of Bawal, the man their father would be so proud of if he were still alive, unable to provide for his family despite his accomplishments. She could see it eating him up inside.

"You don't visit just to tell me I'm not eating. What was the real reason you were here?" she said, attempting to change the topic.

"It's not that important, we need to solve your money issues before I can leave."

"Leave home and return to Bawal, or are you going somewhere?" She said. She quickly finished her water and placed her glass and Gerard's in the sink. "Are you leaving Bawal on a mission?"

"Yeah, something like that. I think it's time that I find purpose. I met a man named Griffen today. He killed the dragon that has been terrorizing Davish."

"Wow, a real dragon slayer? What if the Dragonkin retaliate?"

"That's part of the reason why I'm leaving Bawal for a while. Griffen has asked Wyglaf and me to help him stop the dragons, but we need to recruit some more soldiers."

"You're going to go recruit dragon slayers?" Amily tried to hide the look of concern on her face, but

Gerard's reaction to her made it obvious that she did a bad job of it. "Do you hear how ridiculous that sounds? We're not at war with the dragons. Why would you want to provoke them into terrorizing us any further?"

"It's only a matter of time before they attack. We just want to make sure we'll be ready when the time comes." Gerard leaned against the counter and folded his arms. "Monsters that feel they are superior to us will eventually try to conquer us."

"Is that what Griffen told you? I want to meet this Griffen, especially if you two are going to be traveling with him. I think he might talk a great deal, but maybe he isn't quite backing it up the way you two think."

"He walked into Bawal with a giant dragon's tooth. I think he was speaking the truth."

"He walked into the cave and got that tooth? Was there no one helping him?"

"He killed the dragon, Amily. I believe the story. Bax is no longer terrorizing Davish, and we've heard no reports of the dragon being seen recently."

"So, you were there when he killed it?" Amily also had her arms folded now.

"Why are you being difficult? Of course I wasn't there when he killed it but he brought back proof." Exhausted by the conversation already, Gerard put his hands out hoping his sister would just understand him.

"You're a general in a fancy castle without enough weight to provide for your struggling family. Do you know what I am?" Amily asked, pacing towards the end of the table. Gerard stayed silent. "I'm the second oldest child, trying to care for two other sisters and a sick mother, without my older brother or my father."

Gerard hung his head. He understood what she was going through, but even if he stayed in Bawal it would make no difference "I don't know what you want me to do or say."

Amily knew what she was about to ask was impossible, but she had to try. "I want you to stay, Gerard. Leave the empire behind and come help support our family. I can't do it alone anymore."

"You know I can't leave the empire," Gerard said. "Rebel would never just let me call it quits and leave out of nowhere."

"Just leave," Amily said before she sighed. "You and father are exactly alike, and I've been picking up the pieces ever since he died. You like to think it was you, but you've done nothing." Gerard went to speak, but Amily cut him off. "Don't say another word, Gerard. Please leave. Go find your dragon slayers, hunt your dragons, and don't you dare come back here when you're done." She walked over to the counter and faced the cabinets, tears in her eyes, unable to face her brother knowing the damage she had just done.

Gerard felt it best to not press any further. He stared at the back of her head for a few seconds, before leaving the house. When he made his way back down the long winding stairs, he saw Griffen waiting for him at the bottom, with a bag of supplies in his hand.

"Everything okay?" Griffen asked. He had heard the shouting.

"It's fine. Is everything ready?" Gerard looked down at the helmet that he was holding.

"Yes. I sent Wyglaf and his friend to scout Davish,"

Griffen replied.

"Wyglaf's friend?" Gerard couldn't recall Wyglaf having many close friends.

"Rappez? One of the newer knights in Bawal," Griffen said, as he began to walk towards a carriage nearby.

Gerard walked toward Griffen. "Ah, yes. I think he and Wyglaf have grown close."

"Wyglaf suggested he accompany us on this journey. Davish should have some potentially strong fighters, but I think we'll find more promising fighters in Azuldra. You said you know someone?"

Gerard opened the door to the carriage and let Griffen enter first. "Yes, a mage. He was training at one of the schools there last I saw him. That was a few years ago, so he may have graduated by now. Either way, we can ask around for his location."

Griffen peaked out the window even though they weren't moving yet. "I hope you didn't need anything else from the castle, I packed enough supplies for all of us," he said.

"What you packed is fine, I just want to get this adventure started."

Gerard sat across from Griffen. From his side, he could see his home through the window. Gerard never took his eyes off it, the weight of Amily's words still heavy on his mind and heart.

Chapter Two

Davish was a small town located in the middle of Khroma, that acted as a passageway between the Sanctiveil territories and the start of the Ruebrum territories. Behind the town was the largest stretch of land, where majority of the agriculture on Khroma was cultivated. The Wyndar Mansion stood in the middle of that land. A large carriage pulled up to the front of the mansion, and Wyglaf was the first one to step out. The only other person to emerge from the carriage, was a large man. Taller than Wyglaf though not as wide in frame. His long blue hair hung down to his shoulders and his muscular physique struggled to fit into his leather armor. Around his waist was a large cutlass and the right side of his chest bore the skeleton head sigil of the Bawal Empire.

"The pub said we should try here," Wyglaf

explained. "I have little expectations."

"Supposedly the Wyndar daddy has been hounding the locals to help train his daughter. If he spent his own time training her himself instead of bothering everyone else, she would probably be a fierce warrior already," Rappez laughed and said.

Wyglaf paid the man driving the carriage and then sent him off on his merry way. He turned back and walked past Rappez and up to the door of the mansion. After he knocked, he caught Rappez gazing out into the meadows.

"Fascinating, isn't it?" Wyglaf said.

Rappez shrugged as he looked back at the door. "Just a lot of empty space. A waste, if you ask me."

"Not a waste, every type of fruit you can imagine is grown out here. It's an endless array of food fit for warriors!"

"Yeah, you lost me at fruit. Where's all the beer being made?" Rappez was still staring at the door. He pounded his fist on it. "Anyone in there?"

The door finally opened.

"Can I help you?" Aurora was the one who answered it. Her long black hair was now peppered with gray strands.

"We're here to see your husband, Edgar," Wyglaf said with a smile.

"Edgar is out back with the children. Would you like me to take you there?" Aurora smiled back.

Wyglaf thought it weird that there wasn't a servant answering the door. "That would be great," he said.

"Follow me." Aurora stepped between them, and

Rappez flashed Wyglaf a big smile.

"Don't even think about it," Wyglaf said, his face like a statue.

"Why do you have to be serious about everything? She's hot," Rappez replied, his smile getting bigger by the moment.

"Don't you have a girlfriend?" Wyglaf asked. "The cat?"

"It's complicated. We're spending time away from each other right now," Rappez replied simply. He was studying the back of Aurora's head, wondering if she could hear them.

"Sorry to hear that," Aurora said, as if reading his thoughts.

"Sorry, ma'am. I meant no disrespect by my comments," Rappez said, tightening up as Wyglaf punched him in the arm.

"No need to apologize, I'm flattered." Aurora laughed as she playfully looked behind her. "Is Edgar not paying enough attention to you?" Rappez received another punch after his question. Aurora's smile and friendly vibe left her. "He spends every day he isn't working out here training with the children. I wanted Dawn to become my replacement in running the family business, but my husband took her to see Alencia Skyfall fight in the tournaments in Ruebrum when she was a little girl. She has never been the same since then."

"If he has been training her since she was a little girl, then why is Edgar looking for someone to train her?" Wyglaf asked.

"Then that's why you are here." Aurora stopped

just before the end of the building. It felt like they were walking forever. "You're here to take my daughter away from me."

"Not quite," Wyglaf said. "It's more of an assessment, really."

"It's fine, I knew this day would come and I won't fight you over it. I tried my hardest to sway Edgar, but there is no swaying my daughter now. Him, I could win over, but she is too stubborn to be denied this opportunity."

"She is beyond here?" asked Rappez as he walked to the end of the house.

"Yes, I shall return inside. Please tell Edgar your decision." Aurora walked the other way back towards the front of the house.

"She was nice," said Wyglaf.

"Protective, at least," Rappez added.

"Nothing wrong with that." Wyglaf walked around the corner and found a large backyard, mostly with fruits being grown in a large garden. In the middle, was a large square formed with rocks. In the middle of that were three practice dummies. An older man in blue armor stood next to one of the dummies, holding it tightly as the young woman in front of him landed attack after attack with a wooden stick. To her right, was a young man of similar age hitting one of the other dummies with a wooden dagger.

"Older than I expected," said Wyglaf. "I thought they were going to be younger."

"They look late teens, maybe even early twenties," Rappez noted.

"You must be Edgar," Wyglaf said as he

extended his hand.

Edgar let go of the dummy and accepted Wyglaf's greeting. "Aye, I am. Who might you be?" he replied. "Aurora let you two in, I assume?"

"She did," Rappez also offered his hand. "We were recently at the Davish pub, and we heard that you were looking for someone to help train your kid."

"You heard right, though she isn't much of a kid anymore." Edgar turned back to Dawn and Faris. "Dawn! Faris! Come over here," he waved them over. "I have two men I'd like you to meet."

"Bawal army sigils." Faris put his hand out to shake Rappez's and then Wyglaf's.

"You're a quick study," said Wyglaf with a laugh. "We are from Bawal."

"A pleasure to meet you," Dawn said with a bow. "Are you here to train Faris and me?"

"More of an assessment," Wyglaf crossed his arms. "We're looking to recruit some young fighters for a very important mission."

"Perhaps we can show you what we can do then?" Faris grinned.

"Please do," Rappez put his hand out towards the dummies, urging another presentation.

Dawn and Faris began showing off what they could do.

"What type of important mission?" asked Edgar, he watched Dawn and Faris perform the attacks he taught them, on the dummies.

"I'm afraid that's classified," said Wyglaf. "You're not going to war with Sanctiveil or Azuldra again, are you?" Edgar never took his eyes off the kids.

"No, King Rebel has no interest in such things. Not anymore," answered Rappez.

"Good, I don't want them caught in some large-scale war." Edgar looked up at Rappez, he towered over both of them. "What do you think?"

"The girl is a natural," Rappez said. "Easily could be in any of the top armies."

"The boy needs work," Wyglaf added. "His attacks are clumsy."

Wyglaf walked over, and Rappez and Edgar followed.

"Keep this arm straighter," Wyglaf corrected Faris's stance. "When you attack, it needs to be precise and true. A dagger is a deadly weapon, but the one holding it must be equally as deadly. It takes great skill to master a blade like this."

"Like this?" Faris did it without Wyglaf's help and swung awkwardly at the dummy.

"Close, but keep practicing." Wyglaf turned to Dawn. "Your attacks are thorough, but your balance is off. An opponent with a keen eye would exploit your attacks rather easily. You must learn how to make your movements unpredictable and you must work on your agility."

"I have been working on my speed every day with, sprints and cardio," explained Dawn, ironically out of breath as she spoke.

"Keep at it, you will get it." Wyglaf nodded to her with a smile. He walked back over to Edgar and Rappez.

"Well?" Edgar asked, with a smile of his own.

"I can't take them. Not at their current level,"

Wyglaf said and walked past him.

"That's it? That was enough for your assessment?" Edgar matched Wyglaf's pace easily. "You didn't even see their arts!"

"Unless their arts consist of one-shotting dragons or conjuring beer from thin air, I'm not sure it's going to make a difference," Rappez said.

Wyglaf stood in front of the mansion. The walk back to the front seemed way quicker than the walk to the back. "I'm not saying we will never be interested in them. I'm just saying that they need more practice before I'm willing to take them under my wing," he said. "I'm sorry if that disappoints you. Perhaps, someday, I will return and provide more instruction to help them improve. In the meantime, continue to have them practice daily."

"This will crush their spirits," Edgar said.

"It's up to you to make sure it doesn't." Wyglaf patted Edgar on the shoulder, and then walked away. Edgar stood there, watching them leave, defeated.

On the way back to their carriage that was stationed near one of the farms to gather food for their journey back, Rappez couldn't help but break the silence.

"I didn't want to question you in front of Edgar because it seemed like you made your decision, but I think you made a mistake not taking that Dawn girl." Rappez said, as he grabbed an Arrett off a nearby bush and took a bite. "She's got a ton of potential."

"I saw what she was capable of. But right now she just isn't ready to be fighting people, let alone dragons. I have no doubt she'll be a formidable warrior one day soon. Today is not that day."

Chapter Three

The barren red landscape just before Ruebrum became known as the Dragon Faux after the Strages, the most brutal slaughter of humankind known to man. The Faux became home to the lizard-like monsters known as the Dragonkin. Their creation was also part of the aftermath of the Strages. Led by the Highborn family for the last one hundred years, the fierce beasts tripled in number since their evolution.

Among the Dragonkin, was one by the name of Aerok Doomcaller. A young aspiring warrior belonging to the clan of Brakus Thunderbone, Aerok was the second strongest physical specimen among the dragons. Only Brakus himself could best him in one-on-one combat. His large frame made him stand out among the other Dragonkin, and the green skin of the upper half of his body was a trademark of his family bloodline.

The ambitious Dragonkin often led their hunts and contributed the most to the Faux's expansion in recent months. In order to avoid overstepping their boundaries and ruining their relationship with the humans, the Dragonkin stopped expanding. This particular day saw Aerok storming through the Faux, demanding an audience with Skye Highborn, their leader. The Dragonkin walked on four legs and the bigger ones shook the ground when in a hurry. Skye knew he was coming before he entered his tent.

The tent was located in the middle of the Dragon Faux and was much larger than an average human tent, to fit the large frames of the Dragonkin. Skye often spent his days in this specific tent, planning and organizing the next steps of the Dragonkin. A large red stone table was in the middle of the room with small figures. Though it looked like a war table, it was simply their means of planning out expansion. Without taking his eye off the figure he was holding, Skye addressed Aerok's sudden presence.

"Young Doomcaller," Skye put the figure down on his side of the table. He spoke in the tongue of the Dragonkin. "To what do I owe the pleasure?"

"Do not waste your time with formalities, my Lord." Aerok spoke out. His attention didn't go to Skye, but instead to the massive physical specimen that stood to the left of the table. Brakus, his clan leader, barely fit inside the large tent. His tail was touching the wall of the tent, and his head barely missed the top. "I came to you with news of a fallen friend."

"Avernax," Brakus answered without casting a

glance at Aerok, obviously aware of what had happened.

"You knew?" Aerok placed his hands on the table. "Why didn't you say anything? I just received the report from Kol. He just found out."

"It's of little importance, really," Skye said dismissively. His nonchalance infuriated Aerok. "I told Avernax not to leave the Faux, but he refused. He chose to live among the humans, killed some of them and now everyone is surprised that the humans murdered him."

"With all due respect, murder is still murder." Aerok clenched his fists. "They still murdered one of our brothers!"

"A brother who disobeyed orders!" Skye slapped one of the figures off the table as he yelled. "Everything I do is to protect our people, ensure our future. By going against my orders, Avernax knew what the consequences could be."

"Why are you so afraid of them?" Aerok growled as he spoke.

"That's enough," Brakus intervened. "You will speak to Lord Highborn with respect."

"I have the utmost respect for Skye and his lineage. What I don't understand is why all of the Highborns want to co-exist with the humans." Aerok banged his fists on his own chest. "We are the superior race! This world is ours for the taking, they can't stop us if we so desired it!"

"The humans have been here for thousands of years. They have survived meteors, demon invasions, cataclysmic events such as the Strages, the evolution of their own kind and the existence of magic and monsters. Do you think they can't survive our wrath?"

"I do. We fly the skies and breathe fire! They have no answers for what we can do to them," Aerok said. "If we attack them, especially now that they think we're not a threat, we could wipe them out in a single day. Our high dragons have grown in number, size and strength. The most recently born are some of the most advanced we have ever seen. The humans would not know what hit them!"

Skye's tail slithered over to the piece he knocked off the table and picked it up, placing it back in his hand. "The council and I have discussed this for years," he said. "We have discussed all of the arguments you have right now. War with the humans is not the answer. While you think we would have the upper hand and the unpredictability of it all would be to our advantage, you fail to realize that it goes both ways. Our knowledge of the humans is few and far between. We know their habits, we know where they stay, we know what they eat and drink. Their arts and magic, however, are unpredictable. Super speed, super strength, and some of them can even match our abilities of flight without wings. They know what we are, savage beasts who fly and breathe fire, but the truth is, our large frames make it hard for us to fly for extended periods of time. Our high dragons, though stronger and smarter, are still too few in number for an all-out war."

"Then we wait," Aerok said. "We wait until we're more knowledgeable, until we have more high dragons, more numbers, and then we get revenge for Avernax!"

"Aerok," Skye let out a sigh. "War with the humans is out of the question. They think of us as savage beasts, but a peaceful approach is the solution. The council truly believes that. If we want to expand and evolve further, we need to live alongside the humans."

Aerok slammed his hands onto the table. "I can't accept that!" he yelled. "There is no reason for it!"

Aerok turned violently, his tail hitting the red stone table as he stormed out of the room.

"Keep an eye on him," Skye said without taking his eyes off the tent entrance. "He's too valuable to lose, and we can't have him starting a war with the humans."

"Understood." Brakus walked out after Aerok.

Chapter Four

The mage school, Cresrein, located on Azuldra's main island just before the castle, was the best known mage school on Khroma. Azuldra was home to Palin Syden, one of the most powerful and well-versed mages ever born. He was the one who asked King Arakai if he could set up the school, and soon many strong mages filled the Azuldra army ranks. When Griffen and Gerard arrived, there were numerous kids, teenagers and some young adults outside training in magic. A group of people in red robes were standing closest to the entrance, shooting fire balls at flame-resistant dummies. Griffen walked ahead of Gerard and approached the counter. A young blue-haired woman stood behind it. She had glasses and a yellow robe on, similar to the red robes outside. On the right side of her chest was a blue medal. Griffen assumed it meant her rank, but without knowledge of those ranks he wasn't sure if she was skilled, new or somewhere in-between.

"Hello!" she greeted them. "Are you here to sign up for the next semester?"

"Actually," Griffen turned to Gerard. "I believe we're looking for one of your students."

"Grimoire Tide." Gerard added, assisting Griffen since he hadn't told him the person's name yet.

"Oh, Grimoire..." the woman said and hurriedly looked through some papers in front of her. Her sudden frantic scrambling concerned both of the knights. "We don't have any recent records of Grimoire. You see, he left this school a few months ago and never returned."

"Are you sure? I can't imagine Grimoire leaving, I thought he loved it here." Gerard rubbed his face, wondering what happened that would drive Grimoire away.

"A falling out," a voice came from behind them. A tall man in a blue robe with short blonde hair and bright blue eyes approached them. "Grimoire left a few months ago because he and I had a falling out."

"You must be Palin," Gerard said. "Grimoire told me a lot about you and what you're capable of."

"Grimoire was one of my most talented students. The problem was that he refused to learn at the pace that I set for him, which was the safest and most advanced guidelines I could provide. Yet he wanted to learn more and wanted me to teach him some of the most advanced magic I had. By school regulations, these were spells I could not teach any student, therefore he left to find his answers somewhere else."

"Do you know where he went or where he would go?" asked Griffen.

"Unfortunately, I do not. This was quite a while ago, so he could really be anywhere on Khroma by now. I did hear he was last sighted near Davish though, and that he supposedly frequents The Drunken Way, a pub in Davish." Palin folded his arms. "Mind if I ask what you need him for?"

"I'm recruiting some knights and warriors for a special mission," explained Griffen.

"I've known Grimoire for quite some time," added Gerard. "I feel that he would be a fine addition for this squad."

"He would definitely help strengthen any team," Palin said of the mage. "However, his conquest for new magic might lead to a "no" from him. Might I suggest another mage who trained alongside Grimoire and showed just as much promise?"

"It can't hurt to meet the man," Griffen said directly to Gerard.

"I suppose, though I would still like to try to find Grimoire before we make any decisions." Gerard said and nodded to Palin, who guided them outside to the people in the red robes.

"Rex!" Palin waved down one of the mages. A tall man with red hair and red eyes walked over. "This is Rex Amador."

"A pleasure." Rex said as he put out his hand and shook both Griffen's and Gerard's.

"They are friends of Grimoire," Palin explained. The mention of Grimoire's name made Rex's face turn serious.

"Did something happen to him?" Rex asked.

"Not that we know of. They were looking for him," Palin said.

"Have you heard anything?" added Gerard.

"I haven't seen Grimoire in a few months."

Rex had more to say, but Palin cut him off. Griffen took that as a sign that it was a touchy subject. "Why don't you show them what you can do, Rex? Everyone! Please make room for Rex."

The rest of the mages did as their instructor commanded. They cleared the training ground and Rex set up in front of one of the dummies. "Grimoire is somewhat of a rival to Rex," Palin said.

"I gathered that," Griffen said. "Why so much bad blood among mages?"

"They trained together since they were boys, but Grimoire always seemed to have the upper hand. Grimoire's sudden departure with no warning or goodbyes left a sore spot with a lot of the mages who train here. Especially because he was so good," Palin explained. "He taught them a lot and helped them improve."

Rex set his feet and spread out his arms. His fingers began to ignite with fire. He threw two fireballs at the dummy then slammed his hands together, causing the fire to explode a second time. He then clenched his fists and brought his arms back as fire swirled around him.

"Stand back a bit." Palin put his arm out to force Griffen and Gerard back and out of harm's way.

When Rex's arms shot forward, a large blast of fire surrounded him and filled the training area, and then dissipated before it hit anyone standing around. The other students cheered and clapped at Rex's demonstration. He walked over, slightly out of breath and sweating a bit from the heat.

"What do you think?" Rex said with a smile.

"Impressive," Gerard said.

"We have no doubt you are skilled," said Griffen. "What other types of magic do you know?"

"Rex is a specialist in fire magic. We've created a goal plan for him that will have him completely master the element before branching out into others. Too many students waste their unique gifts pursuing a little bit of everything, I wanted to make sure we didn't make that mistake with Rex." Palin nodded and placed his hand on Rex's shoulder. "You just witnessed the results of that training."

"Seems to have paid off," said Gerard. "If I'm not mistaken, Grimoire was mastering water magic last time I spoke with him."

"That settles it then," Griffen said of this new found knowledge. "I cannot take Rex."

"Are you serious?" Rex's voice went louder than he intended and drew the attention of the other students.

"May I inquire as to why?" asked Palin, his grip on Rex's shoulder tightening to calm him down.

"What we plan to do, it requires more water than fire, and a wider knowledge of spells and magic," Griffen explained. "It has nothing to do with Rex's talent. Fire won't aid us in this journey, unfortunately. Thank you for all of your help and insight, we will go to Davish and try to find Grimoire."

"I see. Very well then. Good luck in your search," Palin said simply, nodded to them once more, and then turned away from them with Rex, who was still visibly upset.

"Fire would do nothing to the dragons," added Griffen as he and Gerard made their way out of the school.

"Yeah, it would be pointless to bring a fire mage. Besides, if we can find Grimoire, I know that I can talk him into joining us," Gerard replied. He stopped short just a few feet from the school. "Looks like Wyglaf and Rappez finished their part. No new people with them though."

"No luck?" Griffen asked as they approached.

"We found out about the Wyndar family, apparently the dad wants his daughter to be a fighter," Rappez said.

"Did you check them out?" asked Gerard.

"Dawn, the daughter, shows a lot of promise. Rappez picked up on it right away but after my evaluation, I'm not sure she's ready to be fighting dragons yet." Wyglaf sighed. He wasn't used to traveling this much outside of Bawal and sounded more tired than anything.

"The Wyndar family lives in the mansion in the Davish fields, correct?" Griffen asked the question in a way that implied he already knew the answer.

"Yeah," said Rappez. "They must be loaded."

"Then we will return there after we check Davish for Grimoire," Griffen said as he walked past them. They all matched his pace and walked beside him.

"Return there? Are we already that desperate for

warriors?" Wyglaf asked, slightly insulted.

"We will take Dawn if we must. I'm more interested in his money," Griffen said with a smile.

"I like this plan," Rappez added with a laugh.

"We take Dawn and have her father pay for supplies." Gerard rubbed his chin as they walked. "It is pretty brilliant."

"It will be a win, win," added Griffen. "You said she shows promise?"

"She does," Wyglaf answered.

"According to Gerard, you're the best trainer in Khroma. I'm going to put you in charge of not making her a liability, and instead making her one of our strongest assets."

"I think I can handle that," Wyglaf said with a smile of his own. "She had another young man training with her. Depending on his art, I believe I can work with him as well. Turn him into another strong addition to our team."

"Sounds like a solid plan," Griffen said. "First, let's find the mage."

"Or something to eat?" Rappez said with a grin.

"We are in Azuldra, I heard the food here is amazing," Wyglaf said. "A rest would be beneficial to an old man like me."

"Can't hurt to refuel first, I suppose," Griffen said. "Let's eat and then head to Davish."

After eating, the knights spent some time traveling from Azuldra to Davish, getting off their carriage just before the large city. Davish was built on neutral ground by the Halstar family, who were famous builders on Khroma. It acted as the meeting point for all of the kingdoms.

Before reaching Davish, the group of aspiring dragon hunters ran into a group of bandits stationed just outside. They were surrounding something or someone, it was hard to tell from where they were standing.

"Quite a large crowd. I wonder what they're looking at," Gerard said, looking up to Rappez, the tallest among them, wondering if he could see what was happening.

"They're surrounding a girl," Rappez said, barely able to just see the top of the girl's head.

"We should help," added Wyglaf.

"It's in our path, anyway," Gerard deducted.

"Hey!" Rappez yelled as he walked on ahead. "Why don't you leave the girl alone?"

"Girl?" One of the bandits whipped around as he spoke. "You don't see this monster?"

"Monster?" Rappez got closer and the bandits spread apart revealing the girl to him. She was short with long black hair. Held tightly to her chest, was a teddy bear that seemed to have been through a lot. One eye was hanging off, some stuffing seemed to spill out, and the rest of the bear looked ragged. Clenching it to her chest were six arms in total. Shocked, Rappez took a step back. "She's still just a girl."

"You don't see it? You really don't see it?" questioned another bandit.

"That's about enough of this," Rappez gritted.

By now, Wyglaf and Gerard were by Rappez's side, all three of them had their weapons drawn. As the three reached the bandits, the girl and the bandits all transformed into monsters before their eyes.

"An illusion?" Gerard turned his head to Wyglaf, but saw him as a monster as well. He shook his head and rubbed his eyes. "Hallucination?" He took a step back and they returned to normal. "Back up!" he yelled.

A black darkness began to surround Rappez before he heard Gerard and he backed away just in time. Wyglaf did the same. "Something is forcing them to change," Rappez said.

"It's the girl," Griffen spoke as he finally joined them. "If we don't do something about the bandits, they will kill her."

"We have no range," said Wyglaf. "We'll need to go in one at a time to not mistakenly kill each other."

"I'll go first," said Gerard as he swung his mace around in his hand. "Just call out so I don't accidently hurt the girl myself."

Gerard moved forward quickly, hoping that the effects of the girl wouldn't hinder him before he could line up a target. He was wrong. The moment his foot stepped on the ground within her aura, the world changed around him. He looked back, his comrades had become three large demons with fangs and blood splattered all over their bodies. The closest bandit became a giant worm with yellow eyes and fangs of his own. He knew the bandit wouldn't be that big so he smashed the base of the worm, hoping it was the bandit's chest.

"You got one!" He heard, but it was hard to make out whose voice it was. Gerard shrugged it off and turned to face the next monster. This one was the shape of a human, but much larger in size, about nearly 10 feet tall. His first attack was aimed at the monster's face out of reflex but he knew he didn't make contact with anything on his follow through. What he felt, though, was a sudden pain in his stomach and he was forced to drop down to his knees. He closed his eyes, hoping that would help him gain his senses, but it seemed to have no effect. He looked up at the giant-sized demon and readied his mace to defend himself, but another monster intervened.

"Get out!" the monster yelled and Gerard turned away from the battle and ran. When the grass fields outside Davish returned to his sights, he turned around to see Rappez fighting off the bandit that landed a hit on him.

"That is like nothing I have ever experienced before," Gerard said, sweat pouring off his face.

"What did you see?" asked Griffen, his interest piqued.

"Everything was horrifying, demonic in nature. Like all of my fears were revealing themselves to me at once," Gerard said, breathing deeply. He took another step back just in case. Wyglaf ran in next to swap with Rappez and put down the final bandit.

"Only the girl is left!" Rappez yelled, causing Wyglaf to fall back.

"My turn," Griffen said. "If she attacks me or does anything to me, get me out of there."

"Are you sure it's okay to approach her? Maybe we can communicate from here?" Wyglaf suggested.

"She is just as afraid," Griffen said.

"Plus, it's hard to hear from back here. I could barely make out what you all were saying," added

Gerard.

Griffen started walking towards the girl before the aura took effect. "I'm going in," he said. He noticed that her eyes were tightly closed and she gripped the bear with all of her might. "It's okay to let go, we won't hurt you."

"Stay away from me. I'm dangerous," the girl said.

"We've gathered that and we've also accepted that."

Griffen's words got through to her. The girl had never been spoken to so calmly before. The girl didn't change form for him, but everything around her did. The ground became black and demon hands began to sprout out from beneath. The trees all died in unison, withering and becoming disfigured. More monsters and demons began to emerge from behind the girl. "Can you turn your art off?"

"I can't, I don't know how," the girl said.

Griffen put out his hand to help her up. "We're going to help you. We're going to find a way, but you need to trust me. We will protect you, but you need to protect us too. Can you do that?"

"If I'm going to protect you, I can't touch your hand. It amplifies the effects of my art."

The girl stood up slowly and Griffen immediately realized she wasn't as young as he thought. She was actually quite tall, almost as tall as he was and her arms were all long and fully formed. The black hair hung down just past her shoulders and under her appendage-packed torso, were two very long legs.

"What was I seeing? The girl? Were you choosing to show me that?" Griffen asked, taking a few steps back. The demons were still around them, but not pushing forward.

"I don't know how to control that either. I think that was the product of what I feel or what I think of myself." The woman before him seemed different, yet she still carried the same qualities and burdens.
Griffen took more steps backwards as the woman walked forward. "What is your name? Do you have one?"

"Iria Rain," she said.

"I'm Griffen." They approached the others, but Iria came to a stop just before her aura would affect them. Griffen walked out of it. "This is Gerard, Wyglaf and Rappez."

"You all saved me?" Iria asked. "Why?"

"Didn't seem like a fair fight," said Gerard.

"It looked like you needed help," added Wyglaf.

"Rappez, take Iria to the carriage." Griffen said and handed Rappez a small sack of gold. "You're going to need to rent the carriage, I don't think the driver will escort you with the aura that Iria gives off."

"You want me to drive her back to Bawal?" Rappez asked. He was annoyed by the thought and a little afraid of Iria.

"Yes, return her to Bawal and ask Shadow if there is a way to suppress her aura. If we're not back by the time you complete that task, meet us at the Wyndar mansion. We should be done in Davish by then and the mansion can be our rendezvous point," Griffen instructed. He gave him the rest of the gold he had on him. "Use the rest to get a ride back."

"You got it. I just hope I can ride this carriage without losing my damn mind." Rappez spoke as he started to walk away. Iria didn't move, and he stopped to look back at her. "You coming?"

"Iria, it's okay. Rappez will take you somewhere where you can get help. Try to suppress your aura to make the ride a little less frightening for him," Griffen spoke softly. He nodded to her then put out his hand to lead her in the right direction. Iria sent a nod in their direction and then walked by them toward Rappez. Her brief passing made everything a horror show again for a moment, but then it subsided.

"Do you think that's a good idea?" Wyglaf asked.

"Out of the four of us, Rappez can probably handle whatever it is that she's dishing out," Griffen assured them. "If we can help her and if her aura can be used against the Dragonkin, she could potentially be our most deadly weapon."

"Agreed," Gerard said with a bit of concern in his voice. "I'm just trying to figure out where she came from. Six arms, demon-like aura and a very cold tone to her voice. Either someone is brewing monsters nearby or she's a demon herself."

"If anyone can figure out the answer to those questions, it's Shadow," Wyglaf said. "Hopefully by the time we return to Bawal, he'll have some answers. In the meantime, we need to find Grimoire."

"Yeah, hopefully he can find a way to suppress that aura too," Gerard said as they all started walking towards the entrance of Davish.

Chapter Five

Davish had the largest buildings in Khroma. When the Halstar family built the city many years ago, they always intended for it to be the hub of the new civilization on Earth. A meeting place for people, Dragonkin and all the other inhabitants of Earth. In due time, however, it was mainly controlled by humans. While the pubs and shops were more welcoming of other races, the ones in charge were all human.

When the knights entered the town, they immediately began asking the townspeople where they could find The Drunken Way, the pub that Grimoire supposedly frequented quite often. They got their answer and made their way to the middle of the town. Despite how populated the town was and how busy the shops seemed to be, The Drunken Way seemed to be teeming with crowds of people. There were people enjoying drinks outside the pub, on a porch where numerous tables were set up. Each side of the porch had numerous barmaids attending to guests and some were stationed just outside the pub, in front of the porch, inviting guests inside.

The three knights stood out as they made their way over to the bar. Wyglaf's large frame in the middle of Gerard and Griffen caught the attention of one of the barmaids.

"Can't say I've ever seen you boys around here before. Passing through?" she said with a seductive grin.

"We're actually looking for someone," said Gerard. "A man named Grimoire. Have you heard of him?"

"Oh, you're all friends of Grimmy? Why didn't you say so?" she gushed. She practically pushed the other guests out of the way to welcome them inside.

"Grimmy?" asked Griffen.

"Never heard him called that before," said Gerard. "He must be inside."

"Stephon!" the barmaid yelled. "Stephon! These boys know Grimmy!"

A tall man with long black hair emerged from behind the bar. He had a cup in either hand that he pressed together to mix a drink. He shook it for a moment then poured it in a glass before handing it to one of the men at the bar.

"Send them over!" Stephon yelled back. He placed the two cups he was using back behind the bar, and then grabbed a towel to wipe off his own hands.

"You boys want anything to drink?"

The barmaid removed a man who was sitting at the bar, he appeared to have had way too much to drink considering it was the early afternoon, to make room for the three knights.

"I'll pass," said Griffen.

"A bit early for me," added Wyglaf.

"I'll just take some water," Gerard answered last. He immediately began looking around the bar after placing his order. There seemed to be no one armed or of any threat. Despite the fact that the three knights looked the most threatening, none of the patrons seemed to pay them any mind. Gerard thought it best that they fly under the radar.

Stephon placed the towel on the inside counter that only he could reach, behind the bar. "So how do you all know Grimoire?"

"He's a friend of mine, I haven't seen him in quite some time. He wasn't where I normally meet him and I was told he frequents this bar quite often." Gerard was still looking around the bar as he answered, before focusing on Stephon. "Have you seen him recently?"

"I haven't seen Grimoire in a few weeks," Stephon said. His answer worried the knights. "He's been spending a lot of time in the Ruebrum territories." Stephon readied a glass of water and slid it in front of Gerard. "May I ask why you're looking for him? Three knights of Bawal is a bit excessive for looking for a lost friend, no?"

"We're all friends." Wyglaf went to answer but the response came from Griffen. "Gerard is just a bit closer to him than we are. It's important that we get reunited soon, we have a big celebration coming up and we wouldn't want him to miss the festivities."

"Indeed, a joyous occasion that should be shared by friends!" Wyglaf added, playing along, though doing a poor job of it.

"Good to know. May I ask something of the three of you?" Stephon asked, taking the towel he had earlier and began cleaning one of the glasses with it.

"What is troubling you?" asked Gerard.

"When you do find Grimoire, tell that bastard he's no longer welcome here unless he's returning my medallion," Stephon's tone completely changed to become sterner. "If I find out he sold it off, and he steps foot in Davish again, I'll kill him myself."

"He stole from you?" asked Wyglaf, shocked by the sudden outburst.

Gerard was taking a drink of his water but Stephon yanked the glass away from him. "Get out. Deliver my message to your 'friend' when you find him! Good day!"

Three large men dressed in black stepped out from one of the back rooms and escorted the three knights out. Each one of them held up their hands in surrender as they were pushed out just past the porch.

"Didn't go well, huh, boys?" the barmaid asked.

"Definitely not the way we expected it to go," replied Gerard. "You seem like a legitimate friend of Grimoire's as well. Do you have any idea where he might be? We really need to find him."

"If he's not here, he's in one of two places. Eyrosa, the town just outside the Dragon Faux or at the arenas in Tark. Gambling or stealing," the barmaid sighed. "Grimmy and I go back, the sudden thievery is not like him. I think he's in a bad way and I think he could really use a visit, and a stern talking to from a friend."

"I'll try my best, thank you for the information," Gerard said as he shook her hand and the three knights began walking towards the exit of the town.

"We should go to the Wyndar mansion before we go to Tark," said Griffen. "I know of a man who fights in the arena that would help us a lot in our mission to stop the Dragonkin."

"But we need the Wyndar's money to free him, I suppose?" Wyglaf asked. He then turned to look at Gerard. "Why do you keep looking around?"

"I feel like someone is following us," Gerard answered, turning his head to look behind them. "Maybe it's just my imagination or a side effect from Iria's aura."

"I think you're just a bit worried about Grimoire. Let's go find him," Griffen spoke as he led the way.

A large purple cloaked figure materialized behind them, once they were out of view. Its large Dragonkin body did a poor job of hiding down one of the alleyways in Davish. Though Dragonkin were welcomed here, the beast still felt it necessary to hide after the recent events with Avernax. In the alleyway, was another Dragonkin with a purple robe draped over its body like the invisible one.

"Lord Kol, they were quiet about their intentions for a while," the newly visible Dragonkin said in their tongue. "But then were very clear that they make moves against us."

"Good job, Hatestitch. I will inform Aerok at once."

***

When the knights arrived at the Wyndar mansion, Aurora Wyndar stood outside, watering some of their plants. She recognized Wyglaf immediately.

She greeted them with a smile, even though she knew one day Wyglaf would return for her daughter. "Back again?" she said. "Had a change of heart?"

"More like...a change of strategy," Wyglaf said. He wasn't fully for Griffen's idea, he didn't like using the Wyndar family for their money, but he was excited to see what Dawn could do and what she could add to the team.

"The children are inside for once, you actually came at the one time they aren't training." She stopped watering the plants and opened the door for them.

"It's important to refuel and rest your muscles as well. I'm happy they're not overworking themselves," Wyglaf said, stopping at the door and letting Aurora go in first before he led the knights inside. "I think the same should be said about you. Don't you have people to do this for you?"

She pushed her hair behind her ear before turning slightly towards them. "It's important that I stay active as well, Wyglaf. Though, your concern is much appreciated," she said. "You didn't introduce me to your friends."

"This is Griffen and Gerard, knights of Bawal," replied Wyglaf.

"Oh! You brought the general with you? This

must be important," she said with another smile.

"You actually know I am the general?" Gerard asked, surprised that apparently more people knew than he thought.

"I try to stay well-versed in all the happenings in Khroma. It's good for business to know everything that could help you sway a deal," she said. Aurora stopped in front of the doorway to the kitchen. "There is plenty of food if you all are hungry."

When the three knights walked into the kitchen, they felt awkward. The room itself was gigantic, but they felt they were taking up too much space. There were two cooks preparing meals in the background of a large dinner table where Dawn, Faris and Edgar sat. Dawn was covered in dirt, Faris had bruises on his shoulders and Edgar looked exhausted as he pushed food into his own mouth. Upon looking up to see the knights, he seemed to be rejuvenated. He shot up out of his chair and offered his hand once more to Wyglaf.

"You changed your mind!" Edgar said, gripping Wyglaf's hand tight.

"I have decided to take Dawn along with us." Wyglaf looked back at Griffen who gave him a nod. "Unfortunately, I must also ask a favor."

"Anything," Edgar said immediately.

"In order to fulfill our mission, we will need supplies," began Griffen. "Most of which will be very expensive and since this is a special mission for the King, we must keep it a secret. This means we can't dip into Bawal's treasury."

Edgar's smile was larger than the last time Wyglaf was at their house."You need money? That's it?

I give you money for the mission, you train and take my daughter to become a knight?"

"That's the gist of it," Griffen replied.

"Though I don't want you to think that this is the only reason we're taking Dawn. That man with me last time, Rappez, he and I discussed in length the potential that your daughter holds," added Wyglaf.

"And Faris?" asked Aurora, despite the children being within hearing distance. Faris had remained quiet in his chair as the praise for Dawn continued. He was proud of his friend, but feared being separated from her.

"I..." Wyglaf began but Griffen cut him off.

"We will take Faris as well," Griffen said, his response a shock to both Wyglaf and Gerard, and even more of a shock to Edgar. "Wyglaf is the greatest fighting instructor in Khroma, he will make the boy a fine warrior."

"I don't know how else to express my thanks," Edgar said, practically in tears. "This means so much to us."

"Besides money we also have some old family heirlooms you might find useful. It's mainly weaponry and some armor that we will never use. If you all can benefit from some extra gear, you're free to take whatever you like," Aurora intervened. She opened a door to the left of the dinner table that led outside. "There is a shed behind where you saw the children training the last time you were here. You might as well go take a look while the children finish eating. When you come back, you should have some food yourselves, while we prepare the children for their journey."

Wyglaf bowed to Aurora and once again shook Edgar's hand."Thank you for your hospitality."

When the three knights stepped outside, the world around them immediately changed. A darkness swept over the green fields surrounding the Wyndar mansion. "Catch!" a voice yelled as bracelets landed into the hands of the knights. Quickly putting them on, they turned to their left to see Rappez and Iria walking up to them, both with surprisingly big smiles on their faces.

"How the hell did Shadow already have something to negate Iria's art? It's not a strong version, he's still tweaking it, but it's enough to stand next to her," Rappez said and pointed to his own that barely fit on his wrist.

"It's probably still a bad idea to touch me though, so please don't," Iria added. Though sounding much friendlier than earlier, her tone still came off cold.

"The bracelets need to be recharged by magical power every few days, so we'll need to make it back to Bawal before that happens. How did it go with the kids?" Rappez asked and tried to look behind them. "That food smells delicious!"

"Aurora said we're welcome to have some after we check the shed. Supposedly they have some weapons and armor that we can use, since the Wyndars have no need for them. You made really good time getting back here," Wyglaf said.

"Yeah, Shadow knew some shortcuts, and I didn't want to miss anything," Rappez said. "He gave me a few extra bracelets, so if we decide to eat or stay the night, we can keep the Wyndars safe from Iria's aura as well."

"Refueling does seem like a good idea," added Gerard as he made his way toward the shed. It was larger than they anticipated, but everything on the Wyndar property seemed larger than what they were used to, including those who lived in the Bawal castle. "A lot of weapons here."

Wyglaf walked in first and picked up a helmet, inspected it, and then placed it back down. "Not much in terms of armor. Nothing we could use anyway."

"Let's grab what we can, ask if we can eat and stay the night, then make our way to Tark as soon as the sun rises. We can't waste too much time here," said Griffen.

Rappez's eye caught a shiny red object beneath a pair of gauntlets. "Griffen is right, we shouldn't waste too much time here."

Chapter Six

In the morning, Edgar summoned one of his carriages to help the knights get to Tark. This carriage was also much larger than something they were used to, the extra space was a necessity now that their party had grown. Dawn and Faris sat side by side, Dawn had the window seat. Beside them was Iria, trying her best not to make physical contact with Faris. The other knights squeezed in across from them.

"Ready to see the world?" Wyglaf asked with a smile.

"We've traveled to Ruebrum before," said Dawn, with a smile of her own. "We were always forbidden to go to Tark though."

"Edgar didn't seem to protest," said Rappez.

"He knows it is part of our 'growing up'," added Faris. "We're both not children, I hope you all realize that. I mean, sure, we're younger than you four, but not kids."

"I like him," Rappez said with a laugh. "You're going to learn a lot from us old geezers."

"Once we reach Tark, let me do the talking," Griffen explained. "These are not the friendliest people and the man we're after is also not very friendly."

"Are we sure we even want him then?" Wyglaf asked.

"This man has no equal in one-on-one combat. The fact that he has been the champion of Tark for years now is proof of that. He will be a big addition to our team," Griffen said as he looked behind him. "We should have plenty of money to afford him."

Edgar loaded up the back of the carriage with 5 large sacks filled with gold coins. The money hardly put a dent into the Wyndar's treasury.

The large coliseum of Tark seemed to rise into the sky forever. The crimson red walls that surrounded it, were amplified by the sun. Dawn couldn't help but stare for a few moments, as Rappez, Wyglaf, Gerard, Griffen and Faris got out of the carriage.

"Iria and I will guard the gold," Gerard said.

"Leave it to us!" Iria said as she emerged from the carriage, utilizing all of her arms. She was not accustomed to being welcomed by others, so her movements were still clumsy and unnatural.

"The bracelets seem to have given you new life," Griffen said with a smile.

"I just want to help the team," Iria said with a smile of her own.

Griffen nodded to Gerard, and then entered the

coliseum with the rest of the group. The walls inside were also red, though a much lighter shade. While the outside was hot, the inside was twice as bad. Sweat immediately began to form on their brows.

"I wore too much clothing for this journey," laughed Faris. "Had I known, we could've saved time."

One of the patrons asked from behind a desk, his words abruptly ending Faris's laughter. "Who the hell are you?"

In front of him, were different parchments for writing. Some of them appeared to be ancient. Also on the table, were numerous cards with drawings on them and tiny wooden figurines.

Griffen put his hand out to ensure no one would speak before him. "My name is Griffen. I've come to speak to you about one of your gladiators."

"You from Bawal?"

As the group approached the man, they got a better look at him. He was small, hunched over and had a cloak that covered his entire body. Up close, the man was more monster than human. A long pointy nose, sharp teeth and two different colored eyes. On his right eye, was a small metal monocle that protruded from his eye to magnify what he was seeing. In his hand, was one of the pieces of parchment and he did not take his eye off it.

"We are knights from Bawal, yes. You are a goblin?" Griffen answered.

"Keen observation," the goblin said, giving Griffen a look as if he offended him. He then pointed at Dawn and Faris. "Those two don't look the part."

"New recruits," said Griffen. "They are of no

concern to you."

"I'll give you 50 gold pieces for both," the goblin said with a snort.

"They're not for sale!" Wyglaf intervened, stepping in front of Dawn and Faris.

"That's too bad," the creature laughed. "Then what gladiator do you want to see? Do you want to place a bet on their next match?"

Griffen folded his arms as he was now standing right in front of the desk. "I wish to purchase one."

The goblin finally put the paper down. "They're pricey," he said. "You sure you have the money to purchase one?"

"We do," Griffen answered firmly.

Griffen now had the goblin's full attention."You want to purchase it to fight or you want to purchase it to keep?"

"He refers to them as 'it', when they're people," Dawn said, disgusted.

"They are slaves," Wyglaf explained. "In their eyes, they are nothing more than property."

"That's wrong," Dawn said.

"Very, but there's not much we can do about it," added Rappez.

"We could free them," Dawn said as she began to move forward. Wyglaf's large hand grabbed her skinny arm.

"We won't be doing that. This entire coliseum is filled with their soldiers, their workers. We would be completely outmatched and outnumbered," Wyglaf whispered as he explained the situation. "Maybe one day we can convince Ruebrum to crack down on the operations here, but the coliseum brings in too much revenue. It would be a difficult fight."

"We want to keep him. Free him," said Griffen. "How much would that cost?"

"Depends on the gladiator," the goblin snorted again.

"Targen Renke," Griffen said. The mere mention of his name sent the goblin into an uproar. At first he paced back and forth, spit and pieces of what looked like tar began to flail from its mouth. It was visibly angry and upset, but that quickly turned into laughter. The goblin slammed its open palms on the desk in front of it. The parchment, cards and figurines bouncing as he did so.

"You want to purchase Targen Renke?" the goblin tried to speak through laughter. "He's our highest grossing gladiator and has been our champion for years!"

"I stand by what I said," Griffen said, immovable in his decision. All of the concern rested with the others behind him.

"Doesn't seem good," Faris said.

"I hope he knows what he's doing," Wyglaf added.

The goblin grew serious. "20,000 gold pieces."

"20,000?" Rappez stepped forward. "I don't think anyone is worth that."

"You shut your mouth, this has nothing to do with you!" The goblin yelled as he pushed himself up onto the desk. His large feet knocked most of what he was working on, onto the floor. "20,000 gold pieces. Nothing more, nothing less."

"Done," Griffen said nonchalantly, to the amusement of the goblin.

"Done? We don't have that money!" Rappez said.

"We do, in the back of the carriage," Griffen answered.

"That's all the money my father gave you for supplies!" Dawn yelled, Wyglaf still holding her back.

"We'll convince Bawal to supply our campaign. Targen is necessary." Griffen never looked back at them, he just kept his eyes on the goblin.

"You're crazy..." continued Rappez in disbelief. "No one is worth that."

"We have the money in a carriage outside," Griffen said. "Rappez and Dawn will escort your men to the carriage and complete the transaction. Wyglaf, Faris and I will meet the man."

"Heh, very well."

The goblin jumped off the desk and signaled to two men standing on either side of the room. The group didn't even notice them, they were perfectly still the whole time. "Go outside with these humans and grab the money."

The two guards did as the goblin commanded. Rappez, who was still complaining, led the way with Dawn beside him.

"I trust you know what you're doing," Wyglaf said under his breath, as the goblin led the way through the coliseum.

"You'll soon learn that I always have a plan, Wyglaf. I am always one step ahead." Griffen grinned as the words left his lips. "You'll quickly learn that my side is always the winning side."

The goblin walked up to another guard stationed in front of a large metal door.

"No wonder there is hardly any metal in Khroma. It's all being used here," Wyglaf observed. "Between the armor and the doors in this coliseum, it's amazing there is any metal available elsewhere."

"Open the door," the goblin commanded and the guard began to slowly pull it open. Though the door looked like a cell door in and of itself, the two Bawal knights quickly realized this wasn't much of a prison at all. Inside was a large room with multiple couches, tables with clay bottles of wine and water, a few tropical looking plants that appeared to have been taken straight from Azuldra, and a large pool in the back.

"What is this?" Griffen said as he looked around the room.

"When you're a champion for years, you get the perks," the goblin said. He started to leave, but then turned back. "Good luck talking him into leaving."

The guard pulled the door closed.

"Look at all of these women," Wyglaf's mouth was open and he caught himself, quickly closing his mouth and clearing his throat. He remembered Faris was there and that he is to be a role model for the younger knight. Faris, however, had no shame and was drooling beside him.

"Relax, old man," Griffen said with a laugh. "This might be harder than I thought."

As the three knights approached the pool, a tall man with dark brown hair stepped out from it. He wasn't wearing much at all, only small shorts that hardly covered him. Targen was the ultimate physical specimen. His chest and arms appeared as if chiseled from stone, each detail in the muscles of his legs on display as he walked up the steps of the pool and as he dried himself with a nearby towel, the sheer size of his arms enough to send the other gladiators running. Despite the two large knights in front of them, the women in the room never took their eyes off the Champion of Tark. He walked over to one of the tables and drank directly out of one of the clay bottles.

"Targen Renke," Griffen said. "The rumors appear to be true."

"Who are you three?" Targen asked, and slowly lowered the bottle down onto the table. "You here to sponsor a match?"

"Not quite," Wyglaf added.

"We just bought your freedom," Griffen said with a smile. The immediate gasp in unison of the women in the room startled him. "...is that not a good thing?"

"What the fuck did you do that for?" Targen slammed his hand on the table and obliterated the clay bottle. "You think I don't like it here? I'm the champion. You can't buy the champion!"

"Actually, he just did," Wyglaf answered.

Griffen walked over and grabbed one of the clay bottles and shook it before taking a drink. "It's true, I did. It seems every man has a price to the goblin who runs this establishment," he said. "You don't really want to be a slave for the rest of your life, do you?"

"Take a look around," Targen said, spreading out his arms. "You think I'm treated like an average slave?

Why the hell would I want to leave this?"

"You don't want to die," Wyglaf said, thinking it a fair response.

"You don't know a damn thing about me," Targen let out a sigh. "To die in battle, in the arena, is the only glory that I seek! You've taken that away from me!"

"With hopes of glory that would overshadow any glory achieved in this arena!" Griffen responded, putting the bottle down and walking over to Targen. "Sure, you can go on for years defeating all inferior men before you, until the day comes that you're off your game or you're too old to continue doing this and you get bested. You die."

"Sounds good to me," Targen said, practically in Griffen's face.

"And if there was greater glory out beyond these walls? Achievements that no man can say they've accomplished?" Griffen stepped back to make space between them, knowing how dangerous Targen was. "Do you want to be like all the champions before you and suffer a similar fate, or do you want to do something that has never been done before?"

Targen turned around and looked at all the women still in the pool who had become completely silent, intently listening. "Cut to the fuckin' chase. If the reasoning ain't good, I'm going to knock your teeth out."

Griffen didn't take his eyes off Targen in hope of gauging his interest. "My colleagues here, I and a few other knights from Bawal are joining forces to put an end to the Dragonkin."

"What?" Targen bursted out laughing, the women behind him all laughed with him. "You came all the way over here from Bawal, spent God knows how much money on freeing me, just to try to convince me to help you fight dragons?" Targen said, still laughing between words, turned to face the women behind him. "I thought you looked dumb when you walked in, but now I know you're three of the dumbest people I've ever met."

"Where do you think the Dragonkin will attack first once they've decided to take over Khroma? They are literally just a few miles away from Tark," Griffen folded his arms, bringing one hand up to rub his chin. "If I were the one in charge of the dragons, I would just take the nearest city. Ruebrum is too big with too many soldiers, including Alencia Skyfall. The smarter of the two options would be Tark. The coliseum and the gladiators would prove difficult for humans to seize, but the ability to just fly over the arena walls and blow fire? They would wipe this place out in mere moments."

"Is that how the champion of Tark would want to go out?" added Wyglaf, following Griffen's lead.

Before Targen could respond, the door once again slowly opened. The goblin came back in.

"I need you in the main lobby, now," the goblin snorted. "I have a problem and I think you're related to it."

"Us?" Griffen asked.

Surprised, Griffen and Wyglaf followed the goblin. The guard left the door open.

"He's a free man now," the goblin said. "Leave it open and go find another post."

The guard nodded and left with the goblin. Targen stood there silently for a moment, turning to the women who were still concerned for the future of their champion.

When Griffen, Faris and Wyglaf entered the lobby, they immediately paused at the doorway. Standing in front of the desk were two large Dragonkin. One had a purple cloak draped over his head and back, the other had leather armor covering its body and long snout. The one with the purple cloak was speaking to the goblin when they entered. He pointed at the Bawal knights as he spoke. The only thing that made sense was "Gnar," which the knights assumed was the goblin's name because it was mentioned repeatedly.

"You speak Dragonkin?" Wyglaf asked the goblin. The Dragonkin stopped talking when he spoke.

"Yeah," the goblin replied. "These two say they followed you here. They want to have words."

"You will have to translate for us," Griffen said.

Gnar plopped down into his seat. "Can't do that. I can't leave the arena."

"I don't see why you would need to," began Griffen.

"They don't want to talk in here, they want to talk outside," Gnar explained.

"Oh," Wyglaf looked at Griffen and the two exchanged a glance. "They want to 'talk'."

Before the two parties could exit, a tall man with long brown hair tied up in a ponytail, pushed his way through Griffen and Wyglaf and slammed money on the desk in front of Gnar.

"Damn it! Can't you see we're handling business

here?" Gnar jumped out of his seat again. "The hell is this?"

"Coin. Enough to wager on the champion!" the man proclaimed. "I won it fair and square in the pits, betting on the matches there."

"Fair and square?" The goblin snorted again. "You don't do anything fair and square, Grimmy."

The mention of his name brought about another glance between the two Bawal knights. Unfortunately for everyone involved, it also garnered the attention of the Dragonkin. After saying his name, they began to ask questions in their language again. Gnar simply nodded, looked around the room then jumped back up on the desk. He grabbed the bag of coins that Grimoire just dropped on the desk.

"Not the type to turn down money, especially yours, Grimmy, but I can't take this and you need to leave right now," the goblin said and pushed the bag back in Grimoire's direction. It turned its attention to Griffen and Wyglaf. "You two need to get out also."

The guards began to approach Griffen, Faris and Wyglaf, but the three just pushed forward and walked out of the arena. Grimoire followed them out.

"You three know those dragons?" Grimoire asked.

"No, we were looking for you though," Wyglaf replied. "Why do they have so much interest in you?"

"I stole from them. That's how I really got enough money for this wager." Grimoire's words caused Griffen, Faris and Wyglaf to stop walking, but Grimoire didn't stop. "Why are you so surprised? Everyone has to steal to survive on this planet if you're not part of an army."

"The dragons wanted us outside. I thought it was to fight," Wyglaf said, looking behind him. "Why haven't they come out yet?"

When Wyglaf turned back to Grimoire's direction, he saw the mage jump backwards. A wall of water formed in front of him and shielded him from an attack that was only made visible by the swipe through his water wall.

"An invisible enemy?" Griffen questioned.

"Seems that way," Wyglaf had his sword and shield ready. "Stay close to me."

Grimoire backed up and joined the knights. The stealthy Dragonkin revealed itself. Slightly smaller than the two that were just inside the arena, this Dragonkin also had a purple cloak. In his hand was a long dagger, with a green substance dripping from it.

"Drake Hatestitch," said Griffen. "One of the deadliest Dragonkin assassins. He can turn himself and anything around him invisible, but he can only do one at a time."

"How do you know all of that?" Grimoire asked, his hands ready to shoot water at their opponent.

"I'll tell you more about that later," Griffen turned around. "I heard noise from the entrance of the arena. The other two must be coming, now that Hatestitch revealed himself."

When Grimoire joined Griffen in looking at the entrance, they were both surprised by what they saw. Out walked the champion of Tark himself, Targen Renke. In both hands, the tails of the Dragonkin they saw earlier inside the arena. He dragged them across the dirt floor. Two heavy to throw both, he let go of one and tossed the other by its tail over near Hatestitch.

Furious, Hatestitch vanished once more and his movements could be heard beside the knights. Before he could reach Targen, Faris also vanished in a flash of light as he moved between Hatestitch and Targen. Removing his dagger from its sheath, Faris brought the blade up in a diagonal motion and felt it connect with the skin of the beast. Dragging the blade through Hatestitch's face, Faris made an incision just below Hatestitch's right eye and pulled upward across his snout. Yellow and green blood began to pour down Hatestitch's face as he became visible for a brief moment before vanishing again and leaving them.

"Should we pursue?" Faris asked, the blood left on his dagger a symbol of his first true victory.

"That quick movement was your art?" asked Wyglaf.

"Yes, I can run and move extremely fast," Faris clarified.

"Try to follow him and scout ahead. Meet us back at the Wyndar mansion as soon as possible," said Griffen.

"You got it," Faris said as he dashed away.

"We saw everything from a distance, but it was all over by the time we got here," Gerard was walking towards them with Iria, Rappez and Dawn nearby. "What was that all about?"

"We were followed by the Dragonkin and they tried to pick a fight with us," said Wyglaf. "I imagine those weren't the only three on our tail."

"Did the goblin's men come out for the money?"

Griffen asked.

"Yeah, they took 20,000 pieces of gold. I hope that this guy was worth it."

"He is, as is he," added Griffen. Wyglaf stepped aside to reveal Grimoire standing behind him.

"Grimoire!" Gerard walked over and embraced his old friend.

Grimoire looked past Gerard at Griffen. "Good to see a familiar face. What have I gotten myself into exactly?"

Gerard grinned. "I suggested you to Griffen, saying you would be a fine addition to this team. Was I wrong?"

"No better mages in Khroma, at least in my opinion," Grimoire laughed.

"We're going to bring the fight to the Dragonkin and I heard you're good with water magic. Are you up for the challenge?" Griffen said, with a smile of his own.

"Does it make me a knight?" Grimoire asked.

"A Dragon Knight of the Bawal Empire," Gerard confirmed.

"Becoming a knight without working for it, and getting to partner up with Gerard. It's hard to refuse a chance like this!" Grimoire said as he patted Gerard on the shoulder. "I look forward to this opportunity even if it's a fight against all odds."

"You don't think we can do it?" Wyglaf asked.

"I just came from the Dragon Faux. Those Dragonkin were looking for me because I stole some of their things to make enough money to bet on a gladiator match. The high dragon that was recently killed in Davish was not the last of them. They have more than five of them from what I saw, and a ton of regular Dragonkin all over. I'm not sure how I didn't get caught."

"It's important that you didn't, important that Faris landed an attack that wounded one and sent it running, important that I single handedly defeated the aforementioned high dragon," Griffen looked around at each one of them as he spoke. "All of those moments show that we are capable of hurting them, that we can rise up against them and actually stand a chance. As our numbers grow, so do our chances of winning this fight, despite the odds."

"I see why you follow this guy," said Grimoire.

"So the question is," Griffen ignored everyone else and looked right at Targen. "Are you coming, Targen?"

"It did feel good to beat the shit out of something that wasn't a human. And this idea of defeating all of the dragons in the Faux is one of the dumbest things I've ever heard in my life," Targen began. The other knights all looked at each other. "But you weren't kidding about the glory to be had here. I'll help you kill these dragons but after that, you have to let me return to Tark, or at least go off on my own."

"Deal," Griffen said, putting his hand out, but Targen walked past him.

"Where to next?" asked the now-former Champion of Tark.

Looking down at his own hand in slight embarrassment and disappointment, Griffen spoke. "Return to Davish. See if anyone heard anything. We know now that some Dragonkin have made their way

North. If the ones we encountered weren't the only ones, then we might have more trouble on our way back to Bawal."

"Let's move," Gerard said. His words caused everyone to head toward the carriage.

"Rappez, wait," Griffen said as the other knights went on ahead.

Rappez turned to face Griffen. "What is it?" he asked. He assumed Griffen was not pleased with his reactions when he made the deal for the price for Targen, but the topic never came up.

Griffen revealed another bag of gold he had on him. "I need you to return to the Wyndar mansion one last time," he said. "If the Dragonkin cut through the fields on their way to Davish, or even worse, Bawal, then we need to know. With Faris heading south, we need eyes on the Wyndars as well. They could be in danger."

"I'll handle it, no problem," Rappez said and took the gold. "Is the gold for the journey there?"

"Yes. There is extra in there for food, but I'm sure the Wyndars will accommodate you. Stay there until we arrive. We will check Davish and then go there, before we return to Bawal."

"Gotcha. You can count on me," Rappez smiled.

"Good. Make haste." Griffen walked away toward the carriage.

Chapter Seven

Davish was not the same when they arrived. Not even close. Griffen had the carriage stop further out than normal, due to the fact that they could see smoke rising from the middle of the town and bright orange flames danced on the houses they could see.

Gerard hesitated after they exited the carriage. “The Dragonkin beat us here.”

“We have to see if we can mitigate some of this damage,” Griffen said. “Grimoire, can you put out the flames?”

“Depends on how much of that fire has spread throughout Davish. I’ll do what I can,” Grimoire replied. He rushed ahead and the other knights followed.

“Enter through the main entrance, but swiftly go off to the side. Work your way around and meet us in the middle. If you run ahead and go to the center of the fire, we may not be able to protect you while you put out the flames," Griffen said, as he motioned with his hands where he wanted Grimoire to go.

"Sounds like a plan. I'll rendezvous with you all in the center."

With that, Grimoire ran off to the right just as they reached the entrance. He followed the right side of the first house he saw and made his way towards the flames.

As the other knights made their way towards the middle of Davish, a deep voice from a nearby alleyway halted them in their tracks. It was the Dragonkin language, so none of them knew what was being said. When they turned to face the voice, they saw one of the largest Dragonkin they had ever seen. Aerok Doomcaller stood triumphantly, the product of his assault all around him. Standing in front of the large Dragonkin, was an average sized human with dark brown hair and glasses. His clothes were burnt and torn, and Aerok had a firm grip on his shoulder.

"Amazing to find a human that speaks our language," the human began translating in a shaky voice. Aerok continued behind him and he spoke again. "I am Aerok Doomcaller, proudest hunter of the Dragonkin!"

"What do you want?" Griffen asked.

The human translated the English into Dragonkin, then translated Aerok's response. "To survive."

Griffen went to answer, but four more Dragonkin leapt out from between the nearby houses and began to surround them. Gerard readied his mace, Wyglaf his sword and shield, and Dawn her spear. Without any weapons, Iria stood in the middle of the group for protection. Targen raised his fists, the only weapons he needed.

"This is unnecessary, let us talk first," Griffen shouted. Aerok responded, his tone much more ferocious than before.

"Enough talking..." The human translated, but before he could finish, Aerok tossed him aside and ran in. Aerok's weapon was a large sword, with bones surrounding both the blade and the handle. It was massive to accommodate the size of the beast wielding it. Griffen finally drew his sword to block the incoming attack, but Aerok overpowered him and pushed him to the ground. The next attack met Wyglaf's shield, which bought Griffen enough time to gather himself.

"This is bad. We're not prepared for this fight, not yet!" Wyglaf pushed Aerok back, but the large Dragonkin spun around and knocked Wyglaf back with his tail. As he pushed forward, he began to lose it and jump up and down smashing the ground around him.

"Stay away!" Iria yelled as she stood in front of Wyglaf and Griffen. Aerok yelled something to the other four Dragonkin, who then ran off into the middle of Davish.

"We can't let them finish destroying the city," Gerard said.

"I think it's already destroyed," Targen responded.

"Good job forcing them back," Griffen said as he adjusted his armor that had been rattled in the fight.

"We need to get Iria weapons, and then regroup."

"If they head south, my parents and Rappez will be in danger," Dawn said. "We should make our way south."

"Dawn has a point, Davish may already be lost to us," Gerard said.

Targen walked over to a nearby building and kicked the door in.

"What are you doing?" asked Gerard.

"The girl needs a weapon, right?" Targen replied.

Gerard nodded to him and then followed suit. He noticed the back of the building had already collapsed. Under the rubble, he could see an arm.

"Didn't end well for this family," Griffen entered behind him and said. Wyglaf remained outside with Targen, just in case more Dragonkin attacked. "See anything?"

"A sword on the wall, that's it," Gerard said, moving in to grab it. He turned and handed the sword to Iria, making sure not to make contact. "Good enough for now. Do you know how to wield it?"

Iria accepted it and held it awkwardly in her bottom right hand. "Never wielded one before, but I'll try my best."

"It will have to do for now, let's head to the middle," Griffen said. He led the way out of the building, past Wyglaf and toward the center of the town. There were bodies everywhere. Some were completely black from the fire, some missed limbs, others with bite marks half the size of their torsos.

"This was a slaughter," Gerard said as he walked

past the bodies.

"First of many, if we don't stop them," added Griffen.

When they reached the middle of the town, Aerok and four Dragonkin were speaking to each other and talking strategy. The knights hid behind a nearby wall of one of the buildings.

"Wyglaf and I will pressure first. Iria will follow in behind Wyglaf and get them into a frenzy," Gerard said. Griffen had a plan but he felt it best to let Gerard, an actual general of battle, call the shots here. Gerard shimmied to face them as he diagramed the plan on his palm. "Then Griffen, Targen and Dawn, you will enter in and take them out while they're distraught and frightened."

"Good plan," Wyglaf said with a smile as he patted his friend on the shoulder, and then turned to Dawn. "Can you handle taking the life of one of these beasts?"

Dawn looked down at the ground for a moment then up at Wyglaf. "If they keep going south, my family will be in danger," she said. "I will do whatever it takes to make sure that doesn't happen."

As soon as the words came out of Dawn's mouth, Wyglaf and Gerard rushed out into the open. The Dragonkin immediately ran after them, but couldn't see Iria behind Wyglaf. He ducked and put his shield up. Iria jumped off of it and swung at Aerok. The leader of this group of Dragonkin jumped back just in time to avoid the attack and far enough to avoid Iria's aura. The other four were not so lucky, but Aerok did not stay to see or share their fate. He ran out of Davish and headed south, much to Dawn's concern.

There was no time for such distractions or feelings, however, as Iria's aura opened the way for Dawn and Griffen's assault. They joined the fight and took advantage of the distracted Dragonkin. Dawn used her quickness and agility to jump into the center of the beasts, shoving the head of her spear directly into one's throat. The beast roared as green blood sprayed all over the ground. She pushed the spear forward, but the beast wouldn't go down. It grabbed the shaft of the spear and threw Dawn to the dirt ground beneath them. Gerard used his mace and struck the spear's end so hard that it shot all the way through the Dragonkin's throat and came out the other side.

Dawn seized the opportunity and grabbed her blood-covered spear and struck the same Dragonkin in the lower back. It roared and turned to face her, but Iria cut the Dragonkin's stomach open with her sword, all six of her arms holding the handle at once. The beast collapsed in a puddle of its own blood.

By the time Dawn and Iria readied themselves for the next Dragonkin, one had already been killed by Griffen and Wyglaf, and another one was on the ground being pummeled to death by Targen. Gerard, having just helped Dawn get her spear back, was already engaged with the final Dragonkin. The other knights began to press towards it, but the Dragonkin was aware it was the last one left, and used its four legs to run away.

"At that speed, we won't catch it!" Dawn yelled.

"We can't let another one get away!" added Wyglaf.

Suddenly, a blur was visible for a moment in front of the Dragonkin, slicing the Dragonkin's throat open. Its blood rained down before it collapsed to the ground, dead.

"Tried to go as fast as I could," Faris said, with a smile, as he walked over to the knights.

"You went to Ruebrum and came back already?" asked Gerard.

"Here I was thinking I made bad time," Faris continued through his laughter.

"Impressive," Griffen added. "You and Dawn are proving to be fine additions. What's your report?"

"I went through Ruebrum and in and out of the Dragon Faux. If it's an all-out assault on Khroma, the rest of the Dragonkin aren't aware. I didn't see any of them preparing to attack, but I also didn't see the purple cloaked ones that attacked us."

"We ran into Aerok Doomcaller. He must be calling the shots on this campaign that the Dragonkin are on. Unusual," Griffen said. "I know a lot about the Dragonkin, and I will teach you all when I can. Skye Highborn is the true leader of the Dragonkin and if he's not calling the shots here, we might be in for more trouble than I originally imagined."

"But that means not all of the Dragonkin are bad," Dawn suggested. "If it's just this group, then it won't lead to war."

"It all depends on how the rest of the humans interpret this attack. Sanctiveil is close by, as is Azuldra," said Gerard. "If they take this attack on Davish the wrong way, they may think the Dragonkin are coming for them next."

"It might grow our numbers," said Wyglaf.

"If they're not scared," added Faris. "I mean, despite what's happening here, most people wouldn't pick a fight with these things. They demolished Davish in seconds, they could easily do the same to Azuldra and Sanctiveil in minutes."

"We have to show them not to be afraid," Griffen added. "If we can prove to them that we can fight back, then they will support our efforts."

A loud splash of water crashing against the building behind them caused them all to avert their gazes. Grimoire put out the last of the fire.

"All done," he said with a grin. "Harder than it looks."

"Any survivors?" asked Wyglaf.

Grimoire looked down at his hands. Clearing all of that fire took a lot out of him. "Quite a few, I had them help each other and gather up in the pub. We need to send them help and rations as soon as we are able."

"Faris," Griffen said, turning to him. "Go to Sanctiveil and get them to send help to those left in Davish. Meet us at the Wyndar mansion after, we're going to pursue them."

With a simple nod, Faris was gone again.

"If we're going to move, we need to move now," Gerard said. "The sun is going down, and we don't want to have to fight Aerok and the rest of the Dragonkin in the dark."

"Agreed. Especially because we'll have no cover. The Davish fields are wide and we'll be out in the open," said Wyglaf.

"It's true. There are a few farms along the way, but none close enough to the mansion to have cover while we scout," added Dawn. "Once night falls on the fields, we will be easy prey for the Dragonkin."

"Would you be able to lead us on foot, Dawn?" Griffen asked.

"I can get us there, though there aren't any shortcuts from where we are currently," Dawn said.

"Not much of a choice. Let's go," Griffen said, putting his hand out for Dawn to lead the way as they exited Davish.

***

In a similar way to when she would play with Faris when they were children, Dawn led the knights through the forests that borderlined the Davish fields. They could all still smell the smoke and fire from the remains of Davish, and each step through the forest brought more and more anxiety. Especially for Dawn. If the Dragonkin had already made their way through the field, then the two people who raised her, the two people she spent majority of her life with, could be in immense danger.

Once reaching the fields, the knights continued their hurried pace. Faris returned and ran up beside them.

"Quick again," Griffen said through deep breaths.

"Sanctiveil is sending help to Davish," Faris said, slowing his pace to match theirs. He wanted to rush forward and see what was happening, but he made a promise to Edgar that he would keep Dawn's safety a priority over all others. He felt it best to stay close to her side in case the Dragonkin were waiting to ambush them. He was right in doing so.

From the outskirts of the fields and the same forest they just emerged from, four Dragonkin flew out of the forest. Two on either side. One went directly for Wyglaf, the biggest target, and tackled him to the ground. The most unfortunate of the four, met Gerard's mace before he even stood a chance. The impact of the metal mace on the side of the dragon's large head caused it to bust open and the dragon fell in bloody fashion. The remaining two surrounded them. One dropped in behind them, the other landed in a way that separated Dawn and Faris from the rest of the group.

"We'll handle this!" Griffen yelled over the dragon. "Dawn, Faris, go check on your family!"

"We can't just leave you here!" yelled Dawn in response.

"They will be fine, Dawn," Faris grabbed her by her wrist and said. "We have to go check on them!"

Much to Dawn's resistance, Faris yanked her along and they headed for the mansion.

"What if there are more dragons between here and there?" asked Grimoire, his back to Griffen's, his hands up and ready to use magic.

"If that's the case, we just have to hope they can outrun them," Griffen spoke as he eyed the Dragonkin up and down. "These dragons are just fodder."

"Still dragons," Wyglaf added, joining the others and bringing his Dragonkin to the party.

"Heh, three of them, five of us," Targen said. "Not even a challenge."

"You sound disappointed," replied Gerard.

"And if the numbers weren't on our side, we also have a secret weapon." Griffen said, as he nodded to Iria.

"Should we be hiding behind this girl?" Wyglaf asked, his pride taking a hit the last few fights.

"Hiding behind her is one thing. Sending her in first every fight is another," said Grimoire.

"I don't mind," Iria said as she stepped toward the dragon that tackled Wyglaf initially. "It's nice to have a purpose."

She swung her sword in the dragon's direction and it parried it. However, Iria's aura was affecting it. It flew up in the air briefly, crashed to the ground awkwardly and then flew sideways into one of his own comrades. The dragon he barreled into snorted smoke and screamed at him in the Dragonkin language, but Wyglaf slashed its arm, causing it to fly back. Grimoire took the opportunity to create a water torrent that launched him up and over the Dragonkin's head and he landed behind it. Now with a better advantage, he blasted the Dragonkin's back with his water magic and forced him into Griffen who was waiting to deliver the killing blow.

The still-frenzied Dragonkin was an easy mark for the knights who all turned their attention to it. Wyglaf bashed it with his shield, Grimoire drenched it in water and Iria climbed its large frame with her arms and finished it off by putting her sword through its skull. As it fell, she rolled off its body and went over to Gerard and Targen to help them with the final foe.

"She's good," Grimoire said. "Where did you find her?"

"Abandoned. We found her alone on the road to Davish, about to get attacked by bandits," Wyglaf answered.

"Wait, you just found this girl?" Grimoire asked again in disbelief.

"Yeah. We're still learning about her, but she's pretty quiet. Seems to have a whole lot of rage pent up," Wyglaf added.

"As long as that rage isn't directed at us, I'm fine with it," Grimoire said and rushed over to help, but Gerard, Targen and Iria finished the Dragonkin off before he got there.

"We need to get to the mansion and see if Dawn and Faris found anything," said Griffen. "Aerok not being with this group has me worried."

***

When the knights arrived, the front door of the mansion was off its hinges and in pieces scattered on the ground, both inside and outside. Understanding what may have transpired and acknowledging the possibility that the worst may be waiting beyond the doorway, the knights silently made their way inside. Griffen led the way, with Gerard, Targen, Grimoire and Wyglaf just behind him. Iria walked in last. On the way to the main living room, there were blood streaks on the wall leading up to it and blood on the floor.

"There was a struggle," Gerard whispered.

Griffen turned the corner into the living room itself, but it was empty. A nearby staircase was where the blood stains stopped. Griffen turned back and silently signaled to the rest that he was going up. They followed him upstairs, where a few more drops of blood were found. The trail led them to a large bedroom. Inside, they saw Dawn on the floor cradling her mother's body. Tears streamed down her eyes. Faris stood beside her, trying to be strong for his friend.

"What happened here?" Griffen's question was directed at Faris.

The shock was written on Faris's face, but the other knights were impressed by how he kept himself together. "Had to be the dragons."

"Aurora didn't say anything before she died?" Wyglaf asked.

"She was dead before we got here," replied Faris.

"What about Edgar?" asked Griffen.

"Dead, in the cellar," Faris said, fighting back tears.

Grimoire tried to piece everything together, but a few things didn't add up. "How did Aerok beat us here so fast?"

"I don't think Aerok was the one who did this," Griffen debunked. "I think Aerok was the distraction."

"He kept us in Davish and in the field, while someone else committed this murder?" Gerard spoke harshly, clenching his fist. "That bastard."

"He knew we would get here before him, so he stalled us long enough to have the rest of the Dragonkin do his dirty work," Wyglaf added.

Faris knelt down beside Dawn. "I should've ran ahead."

"This isn't your fault," Dawn looked up, a reflection of the innocence and beauty of her mother. "You stayed to protect me, like my mother and father asked you to."

A shadow in the window caught Gerard's eye. "They didn't leave," he said. "They're surrounding the mansion!"

Grimoire moved to the side of the window and peeked out. Faris did the same, on the opposite side.

"I see five, at least, on this side," said Grimoire.

"About the same here," Faris said. "Hard to tell if there are any just below the window."

"Is Aerok there?" asked Griffen.

"How do I tell?" Grimoire replied with a question of his own.

Griffen inched his way to the window where Grimoire was, to take a look for himself. "Aerok is much bigger and has more black markings, like tattoos."

"Got some movement in the forest on this side," Faris said as Gerard joined him.

"He's on this side," Gerard said. His words brought the rest of the group to their window. Grimoire stayed on his side to keep an eye out on the Dragonkin.

Aerok stepped out from the forest and the rest of the Dragonkin on that side turned to face him. He was carrying a large piece of wood that was a dark red color. He spoke to the others in their language before looking up at the window, directly where the knights were watching. He raised the large wooden club in his hand, then used it to point further south.

"He's showing us his next target," Griffen said.

"South from here would be Bawal territories!" Gerard backed away from the window and exclaimed. "We can't let them take Bawal."

"At least we know where he's going," Wyglaf

added.

“Why show us though?” Grimoire said, and he saw no movement from the dragons outside his window.

“He doesn’t intend for us to follow him there. Look at the club!” Faris said as he watched in horror as the large red club started to light on fire on both ends.

Griffen turned to Grimoire. “He’s going to burn the mansion down,” he urged. “Get downstairs and put out that fire before it starts!”

“I need cover if they come in after it,” Grimoire yelled back.

Targen, who had been silent up until this moment, cracked his knuckles and moved his head side to side. “Leave that to me.”

Without saying another word, Targen ran downstairs. Grimoire followed him down. Aerok was waiting at the door when they got down there, he launched the club with such force it ripped through the rest of the doorway and some of the walls before flying in toward Targen. Targen ran forward and slid under the club.The moment it touched the ground, it began lighting the house on fire. Grimoire immediately began to douse it with his water magic.

“It’s not working!” he yelled toward the stairs to warn Griffen and the rest.

Targen, ignoring what was happening behind him, ran straight for Aerok who backed away from the door and began to run toward the forest. As soon as Targen exited the mansion, a massive Dragonkin fist came for his face. He ducked, and wrapped both arms around the dragon’s wrist and flipped him into two other dragons.

"We need to get out of here, probably through the window," Gerard said, looking to see if they could safely land. "The dragons on this side are following Aerok through the forest towards Bawal."

Griffen removed his sword and smashed the window with the handle of it. "Not much time to think this plan over. We have to get out of the house!"

Iria jumped out first, sliding on a piece of one of the mansion's balconies and crashing to the ground. She began to run for the shed with the weapons the knights were free to take from, the last time they were there.

"You go next," Wyglaf said to Griffen. "It's important that you make it out."

"We're all making it out of this," Griffen said. "I'd rather go last and make sure you're all to safety."

"Honorable," began Wyglaf, "but I'm more likely to destroy whatever we're sliding on with my size. Go!"

Griffen hesitated. before Wyglaf turned him around by putting his hand on his back. Griffen exited the building.

"Gerard," Wyglaf called on him next. Gerard nodded to Wyglaf, and then slid down the balcony and onto the ground as well.

"Dawn, I know this is harder for you than it is for us, but we need to go now," Wyglaf said.

"There isn't anything else we can do now," Faris said.

"I want to just look in her face once more, hear her tell us about the past once more!" Dawn wouldn't let go, but Faris eased her off.

"I need you to focus Dawn, please!" Faris said she he helped her toward the window. "You need to make this landing."

"Slide with her," Wyglaf said.

"I'm not sure if I can do that," Faris looked out the window to double check where he needed to land.

"You can do it, with your speed. You can get both of you on the ground like you never even fell out of the sky," Wyglaf patted Faris on the shoulder. "You can do this!"

Faris hugged Dawn tight before backing out of the window and speeding to the ground. The impact made Dawn a little wobbly as she wasn't accustomed to Faris' speed. The two quickly gathered themselves as two Dragonkin bust out from the back of the mansion.

"They were inside the whole time?" Faris asked as a Dragonkin's blade whizzed by his face. Before he could react, Iria ran past them with multiple swords in all six of her hands. She moved so fluidly, it looked more like a beautiful dance than a relentless massacre. The two Dragonkin went down quickly as Gerard pulled both Dawn and Faris back, just before Wyglaf crashed into the ground.

Dusting himself off and clearing his throat, Wyglaf ignored the judgment of his comrades. "We need to get Grimoire and Targen out."

***

"I don't know why it isn't working!" Grimoire shouted as he continued to try to put out the flames.

"Exit through the back!" Targen yelled over the fire.

"What about you? You won't make it through

the front against all of those dragons!" Grimoire suppressed the fire long enough to get a view of Targen. He had a few bruises and the soot was all over his face. "*Wait...*" Grimoire thought. "*Is he actually smiling?*"

Taking Targen's reaction as his answer, Grimoire abandoned the fire and ran for the back door of the house. He dodged some more fire, but tripped on his way out the back door. As he rolled toward the other knights, the back doorway and half of the mansion collapsed from the fire.

Gerard ran over to help his friend up from his knees. "Grimoire! Where is Targen?"

Grimoire got up, but the roll took its toll. He was favoring his right leg. "He went out the front door, we need to go help him!"

"I'll go, catch up when you can," Faris zoomed off. When he arrived in the front of the house, there were Dragonkin bodies everywhere. At least ten. Faris stood in awe as the rest of the knights ran up to them.

"You did that with just your fists?" Wyglaf asked.

"Like I said," Targen smiled. "Not even a fuckin' challenge." He spit on the ground after he said it.

"Yeah, you said that when we had the advantage, but this," Wyglaf said as he looked around. "This is just crazy."

"Are you planning on recruiting any more psychopaths for this mission, Griffen?" Gerard said, both impressed and concerned.

"You say psycho, I say effective," Targen said as he brushed against Gerard's shoulder when passing by. The blood and soot covering Targen left a mark on his armor.

"Either way, we need to get to Bawal. And fast," Gerard added.

Grimoire looked down at his hands. "I don't know any teleportation magic, sadly. One of the only fields I didn't practice in before switching primarily to water magic."

"It's fine," Griffen turned once more to Faris. "Are you up to doing another scouting mission for us?"

Faris looked out in the distance, the burning mansion behind him. "Have to be. Where to now?"

"Though the South borderlines with Ruebrum, there is no way they would go South just to attack a neighboring castle," Griffen began, and Wyglaf and Gerard nodded in agreement with his words. "Coming this far out, they are definitely eyeing up a Bawal territory. My guess? Dreadsmirk."

"It's the most populated and closest of the Bawal territories," added Gerard.

"Exactly, it makes the most sense that they would hit there instead of the smaller, closer towns," Griffen said as he pointed in the direction of Dreadsmirk. "If you cut through the forest there, it should take you to Dreadsmirk, but you need to pass through a town or two on the way to make sure you're in the right place."

"I'll check those towns as well just in case, but it should be easy to tell where the dragons are," Faris said.

"Sounds good, we'll catch up as soon as we can. If you see them, don't engage. Just help as many people as you can. If they're under attack, then get them to safety until we arrive," Griffen said, and removed a dagger from the back of his belt. "Take this with you, it's a bit sharper than what you're using. Don't use it unless you have to."

Faris took a moment to admire the dagger. The handle was gold and the blade looked like it was never used before. It was the cleanest weapon he had ever seen, not that he had seen many in his lifetime. "Thank you. I'll see you all in Dreadsmirk."

"We need to win the fight in Dreadsmirk," Griffen said. "Aerok has been two steps ahead of us the whole way. We need to show him that we're able to defeat them."

Gerard folded his arms. The simple gesture reminded him of his sister and the conversations they had prior to him leaving with Griffen. "I think we shouldn't only go to Dreadsmirk."

"Share your thoughts," Griffen said.

"If Aerok has been one step ahead of us at every turn, I feel like Dreadsmirk is too obvious. He knows we'll go there, meaning it could be another trap," Gerard said. He looked to Wyglaf to approve of his observation. The elder knight was listening intently. "The attack in Tark drew us to Davish, but the destruction of Davish was a distraction so they could attack the Wyndar mansion. Now he points to where he's going and expects us to just follow him there?"

"It does seem suspicious," said Wyglaf.

"I have no doubt he's going to attack Dreadsmirk, but what is he really doing that he doesn't want us to see?" Griffen wondered. He turned to look at the forest. "What are we missing?"

Wyglaf's attention was on the mansion burning behind them instead. "Bawal is home to Gerard and me. This mansion is of meaning to Dawn and Faris, and he probably knew we were here. If my suspicions are correct, he's been following our moves since we got to Davish looking for Grimoire."

"They confronted us at Tark to put things in motion," added Grimoire.

"He has no intention of starting a war just because we're humans and he's a dragon," Griffen said. "He wants it to be more personal, so this war has to happen."

"None of us have family in Dreadsmirk..." Wyglaf said.

"He's going to Diremoore!" Gerard blurted out, sudden concern obvious in his voice. "How did I not see it? It's just beyond Dreadsmirk. My siblings are there!"

"I'll go with Gerard. Iria will come with us. We'll check Diremoore," Griffen began speaking as Gerard already began moving toward the forest. "We'll grab a carriage at the first town we see since I don't think Iria can ride a horse without influencing it with her aura. The rest of you join Faris in Dreadsmirk. If we don't arrive before you're done there, get to Diremoore as fast as possible. Send Faris ahead."

"Understood," Wyglaf nodded to Griffen. "Keep Gerard's family safe."

"Keep Dreadsmirk from the suffering the same fate as Davish," Griffen replied, and they went their separate ways.

Chapter Eight

When the knights reached Dreadsmirk, the entrance to the town was relatively quiet.

"It's quiet, but there are people lined up over there," Grimoire said. "We should take a look."

As they made their way to the townspeople standing outside their homes, Faris appeared before them and started walking beside Wyglaf.

"I checked a few villages on the way, there were no signs of the dragons. They're here though. I told as many people as I could, to stay towards the edge of the town or leave if they could afford to," Faris explained.

Wyglaf readied his sword and shield. The other knights prepared for battle as well. "How many dragons?"

"Well, it was hard to tell. There are a bunch of

purple cloaked dragons, and some were turning invisible. There was a slightly larger one with a marking on his face, that I assume is leading this group," Faris said and took out the dagger Griffen gave him, as they made their way to the center of the town. "There's a large square opening coming up, and that was the last I had seen them."

As they approached, there was a lot of noise pointing them in the right direction. Steel meeting steel and the yells of both dragon and man.

"A fight broke out?" Grimoire questioned as he looked at Targen, the knight closest to him.

"Sounds that way," added Dawn, who had finally gathered herself despite the traumatic event she just experienced.

"If so, whoever it is, they're in danger and we need to help them," Wyglaf said, leading the way as they ran out into the center of the town.

Surrounded by the dragons, were two men. One of the men was holding two swords. He had red hair that went down to just above his chin. His leather armor covered his body from his neck to his feet, but his arms were left bare. The man's physique almost rivaled Targen's and his stance told Wyglaf that his experience was vast. Standing back to back with the dual sword-wielding man, was a boy who looked to be in his teens. He had short black hair, similar leather armor and the sword he was wielding had a black handle with a crimson red blade.

"Looks like they can hold their own," said Grimoire.

"That means they're going to get to have all the

fun if we don't hurry," yelled Targen as he rushed in to help.

The first Dragonkin Targen approached received a fist directly to the jaw. Without concern for his surroundings, another Dragonkin almost blindsided him, but Dawn leapt into the air and came crashing down on it with her spear. Grimoire began blasting the dragons with water, as he worked his way to the middle. Wyglaf followed suit, slicing and shield, bashing his way through.

"Looked like you two could use some help," Wyglaf said to the man wielding the two swords.

"Thanks," the man replied. "I'm Azadan, this is Vallick."

"Nice to meet you," Grimoire added through a grunt, as he pushed back the dragons.

"We've already beaten quite a few of these things, but they just keep coming," said Vallick.

"Have you seen a larger one with more tattoos and no cloak?" Wyglaf asked.

"No, the ones we've fought are all wearing purple cloaks," answered Azadan.

"The one I speak of is called Aerok Doomcaller and he's the one leading these attacks. If he isn't here then, Diremoore may be in danger," said Wyglaf.

Faris finally joined them, dashing through two Dragonkin before joining their side. "Should I head to Diremoore?"

"That was what Griffen was thinking we should do if Aerok wasn't here," said Wyglaf. "We should be fine now, with Azadan and Vallick helping us."

"I'm going, then." Faris vanished before their

eyes, kicking up some dust as he went.

"Super speed?" asked Vallick.

"Something like that," answered Grimoire with a shrug.

"That's a very strong and dangerous art," Azadan said.

"Yeah, we're happy he's on our side," Wyglaf added.

The group's attention was immediately drawn to Targen, who had mounted a nearby Dragonkin and was punching it repeatedly in the face. Dawn was guarding him with her spear. When the former champion of Tark stood up triumphantly, as he does, the blood splatter on his chest and face was more of a trophy than a disgust. "You guys just going to stand there and hold hands the whole time? Or are you going to help me kill these things?"

"Do we have to kill them? Can't we just injure them and lock them up somewhere?" asked Dawn.

"You fuckin' crazy?" Targen exclaimed as he stepped over the dragon he just pummeled. "You think they're planning to lock us up?"

"Until we have more information, I think it's fair to say 'kill or be killed'," Wyglaf said. "It's not pretty or the best way, but if this is the start of a war, then we need to bring it to them."

"Exactly, bring it to them. So, get over here," Targen said, waving his comrades over. "I saw some of them run this way."

"What about the ones here?" Vallick asked.

"You didn't kill those yet?" Targen walked over to them. "Let's do it!"

Targen flew past Wyglaf and planted another fist on an unsuspecting Dragonkin. Vallick joined him, utilizing his red sword to incapacitate another dragon and leave an opening for Grimoire to hit the next one with a pillar of water. The pillar smashed the dragon into the ground then raised it up into the air on a geyser, before smashing it into the ground a second time.

"What's the story behind the sword?" asked Dawn. She and Azadan were further behind, and killed one of the dragons together.

"Vallick's wielding a legendary sword created by the blacksmiths Orik Lagra and Hammerdin Chime. The sword was given to the Halstar family, and was passed on from generation to generation, but no one was able to wield it until Vallick tried."

Azadan's story was interrupted by another dragon, but he sidestepped the attack and slashed it twice with his swords before crouching to the ground to give Dawn an opportunity to deliver the finishing blow. She took advantage of it and stabbed her spear through its eye. "He's still learning to control its power, but he improves greatly with each day of training."

When both of them looked up, a Dragonkin appeared out of thin air and swiped at Vallick with a large dagger. Vallick dodged the attack, but being surprised put him off balance and he crashed to the floor. The concern on Azadan's face caused Dawn to act, and she used her agility to weave through the other knights and the dragons between them. Just as the now-visible dragon went to cut Vallick, Dawn got in between them and blocked the attack with the shaft of her spear. She twisted her arms to force the Dragonkin off balance. Vallick jumped up immediately and stabbed it through the chest with his sword.

"Thanks for the save," he looked back at her with a smile and sad. "You know our names now, but none of you introduced yourselves."

"I'm Dawn," she replied with a smile of her own. The rest of the Dragonkin were all on the ground, dying or dead. The other knights approached them. "This is Wyglaf and Grimoire. The crazy one still punching things over there is Targen. The one with the speed-based art is Faris."

Dawn's introductions piqued Vallick's interest. "Wow, you all are knights of Bawal?"

"A few of us are, officially. The rest were recruited for this mission," answered Wyglaf.

"What relationship do you two share?" asked Dawn.

"Azadan is teaching me how to wield Crimsonious and master my art," said Vallick.

"Ah, another teacher!" Wyglaf said with a smile. "I train the knights of Bawal."

"We have to discuss strategies when this is over," Azadan added.

"In the meantime, we should make our way over to Diremoore to help the others," Grimoire said. "If Aerok isn't here, then I'm afraid Gerard was right in his assumptions."

The conversation was interrupted by a load roar. When the knights turned to face the noise there were two Dragonkins in purple cloaks. One had his hood down, a large black marking surrounded his left eye.

The other, despite having its hood over its large head, had a visible yellow scar down the middle of its face.

"That's the one Faris hit," said Dawn.

"Drake Hatestitch is what Griffen called him," added Grimoire.

"And the other one?" Azadan asked.

"Not sure, but I think it's safe to assume that's Aerok's right hand man," said Wyglaf. "He's not to be taken lightly."

"But he is to be taken," Targen spoke fiercely as he cracked his knuckles. "I get dibs."

"Targen, wait, we should think of a strategy!" Wyglaf shouted, but Targen was already en route. His first wild swing was easily avoided with a simple back step, and the larger Dragonkin put Targen in a headlock. "Why does no one listen?" Wyglaf added with a sigh.

"It's not that no one listens," said Grimoire. "Just Targen, apparently."

The larger Dragonkin shouted something in his language, before throwing Targen to the side. It pounded its chest and roared before proclaiming itself, "Kol, the Typhoon."

"Well, that settles that," said Azadan.

Azadan was next to charge in, with Vallick close behind him. His first swipe was sidestepped by Kol, the second one landed across the beast's chest, but it was unfazed. It spun around, catching Azadan in the back with its tail. Vallick took the opportunity to slash at its back, but the attack was blocked by Hatestitch. Growling in Vallick's face, Hatestitch shook its head to further reveal the yellow scar Faris gave it, then used the pressure it was applying on Vallick's sword to push him aside. It pointed its dagger at Wyglaf.

"They're familiar with you now," Grimoire said with a laugh.

"I don't see why that's funny," Wyglaf gritted out and covered as much of his body with his shield as he could. "Just watch my flank."

Wyglaf blocked the first strike of Hatestitch's dagger with his shield, and then launched a counter attack with his sword. Before making contact, Hatestitch turned invisible.

"Don't worry, Wyglaf, I got this. Just buy me some time!" Grimoire shouted, slammed his palms together and began chanting.

"I'll help!" Dawn yelled, rushing to Wyglaf's side. She swung her spear around in a large circle to ensure Hatestitch wasn't nearby.

Grimoire finished his spell and then raised his arms into the air. Suddenly, it began to rain in Dreadsmirk. The pattering of the raindrops did enough to reveal Hatestitch's location even when he was invisible. "That should help!"

Now with sights on him, Dawn stabbed her spear in Hatestitch's direction, but the beast parried it. His art now useless, Hatestitch thought it best to turn tail and run, so he did. The large footprints were amplified by the puddles forming beneath him as he ran.

"Useless!" roared Kol, though none of the knights understood him. He barreled forward and used his large skull to knock Targen to the ground. He used his left hand to swat Azadan to the side and his right to do the same to Vallick. Now in front of Wyglaf, Grimoire and Dawn, he roared once more. This time he blew smoke and fire into the sky.

"I hope you're cooking up a plan, Wyglaf," Grimoire said as all three knights slowly backed away from the dragon.

Wyglaf held his shield in a protective stance to cover Dawn and Grimoire, who stood directly behind him. "Still cooking. For now, shoot water and try to survive."

"I can do that," Grimoire said as he created a pillar of water beneath him. He shot himself into the air and then put his palms together once more to shoot a direct blast of water at Kol's face. The beast flinched and shook its head. Grimoire floated back down to the ground. "I think I made him angrier than he was before."

Kol ran towards them, removing two large bone swords from his waist. The blades were similar to Aerok's, though smaller in size. Once ready in his hands, the dragon began to spin wildly, his tail and the two swords creating a dangerous whirlwind. The first swing grazed Dawn's shoulder before connecting with Wyglaf's shield. The impact forced him to the ground and onto his back. Grimoire jumped backwards to avoid the attack.

"We need to get Dawn out of there!" yelled Grimoire to Wyglaf, who was still gathering himself.

Dawn was just underneath the attacks. She laid down on the ground to further avoid them but the dragon's tail was close to her on every rotation. Suddenly, the dragon stopped. When Dawn looked up she saw Targen holding its tail with both arms. Dawn tried to get up, but the dragon swung one sword at her, despite Targen halting its progress. Dawn rolled out of the way of the first attack, but Kol anticipated her movements and began swinging his sword where she stopped. Unable to avoid the attack, Dawn put her spear up to brace for impact, but the attack never reached her. Instead, Vallick slid on the muddy ground created by Grimoire's rain, scooped Dawn up in his arms and returned her to her feet.

"Thanks!" Dawn yelled, even though Vallick was standing right next to her. "You saved my life on that one."

"We're not safe yet," Vallick said, stepping in front of her to protect her. Kol shook its tail from Targen's grasp and ran directly for Vallick. "I'll stun it, but you need to be ready."

Dawn pushed her black hair from her face then stood with her legs ready to pounce and the head of her spear pointed forward. "I'll be ready."

Grimoire ran up beside them. "Put your feet in the water I make, Vallick, and I'll provide you the opening."

"Alright," Vallick looked past Kol through an opening between its arms and nodded to Azadan who was ready on the other side. "Now!"

Upon Vallick's command, Grimoire created a bridge that went over Kol's head. Vallick put his feet into the water, as Grimoire instructed, and the current had so much force it shot Vallick over the Dragonkin and onto the other side. Right as Vallick landed there, Azadan rolled in the opposite direction to get in front of Kol. The dragon attacked, but Azadan parried each attack with his swords.

While Kol was distracted, Vallick clutched the handle of Crimsonious, the already crimson blade turning an even darker red before Vallick raised it and shot a blast of red energy into the dragon's back. The attack forced Kol to drop his swords and stagger forward. Azadan seized the opportunity and went to stab both of his swords into the dragon's stomach, but Kol was ready. He grabbed both of Azadan's swords with his large, bare hand and once again roared loudly. He threw Azadan aside, but caught the tip of Dawn's spear in his throat. Dawn used the spear to climb up the dragon's large frame and removed her spear for a second attack, but Kol threw her off with his left hand.

"It can't have much more left in the tank," said Grimoire. "Stabbed its neck, opened up its back, can't it just die already?"

Feeling the effects of Vallick's attack on its back, Kol began to roar, swinging his arms and tail wildly.

"These things don't have much of a structured offense," observed Wyglaf.

As it spun in the opposite direction of the knights, Targen planted another fist on its jaw and then added two more punches to the stomach. The attacks caused Kol to hang his head over and grip his stomach with both hands. Targen placed two more punches on Kol's face, but the dragon threw both hands forward and backhanded Targen away. Another wild swing toward the other knights found a waiting Wyglaf, who swatted Kol's attack before stabbing his sword diagonally into its stomach and up towards its chest.

Kol roared once more and grabbed at Wyglaf's back before falling awkwardly to the side.

"That has to be it, right?" asked Azadan, staring down at the dead dragon.

"If it gets up from that, then I don't know what else to say," replied Wyglaf.

"Look," Dawn said, pointing to one of the houses. "The people are coming out!"

The townspeople that were still in their houses began to emerge and those that Faris saved by taking to the outskirts of the town entered the square, still keeping their distance from the dead dragon. They began to clap and cheer. Grimoire waved and raised his arms in response, and Targen nodded as if this was something he was used to, but Wyglaf remained all business.

"Enjoy the moment, but we need to get to Diremoore. We can't wait here," Wyglaf said, turned to Azadan and offered his hand. "Want to come with us?"

Azadan accepted the gesture. "I think Vallick and I should remain here to help clean this mess up, and just in case more dragons show up."

"Understood," Wyglaf shook Vallick's hand as well. "Thank you for the assistance."

"Anytime," Vallick responded.

Chapter Nine

Diremoore was similar to Dreadsmirk when the knights entered, but there were no people lined up on the outskirts of the town. Instead, they all remained inside. Griffen saw no signs of dragons when they entered and Gerard began to rush towards his home. Iria stayed close to Griffen's side.

"He shouldn't run in by himself," Iria said.

"Agreed, but when our family is in danger, it makes us act without thinking," Griffen replied. "Do you have family, Iria?"

Iria walked ahead of Griffen now, checking alleyways and building windows. "No, none that I know of. I can't recall the earlier years of my life," she answered.

"You have family in the Dragon Knights now," Griffen checked the opposite side of the street. "Don't forget that."

Iria couldn't help but smile, despite the eerie situation they were in.

"Griffen!" The loud voice was Gerard's and it came from the center of the village. Griffen and Iria exchanged glances, before running towards it. They found Gerard standing in front of five Dragonkin who were guarding his home. Aerok was not among them, but revealed himself shortly after. He didn't stand in front of Gerard's home, but instead stood in front of one of the nearby houses.

"Family is important," the Dragonkin began, though the knights could not understand him. "I hope mine come to understand my actions here today."

Aerok pointed at Gerard's home. Then turned and pointed to the house behind him. He looked right at Gerard as his eyes began to turn red, then blew fire all over the house behind him.

"Save them, or save your family?" the beast shouted in his language before roaring into the sky, his fellow Dragonkin joining his cries.

"Iria and I will help the people in the building, make a path to your family!" Griffen ran toward the burning building.

Faris whizzed past everyone and slid beside Gerard.

"Great timing, Faris," Gerard said as he readied his mace.

"That's kinda my thing," said Faris with a smile, the dagger already in his hand.

Griffen shielded his face, before kicking open the door to the burning building. Iria used her extra arms to navigate her way to a nearby set of stairs where she heard screaming on the floor above.

"I'll check the top, you check the bottom!" she yelled as she went up the stairs.

"Be careful!" replied Griffen.

Upstairs were three young girls. The moment Iria entered the room, two of the girls began to cower in fear against the nearest wall of the room, ignoring the fire.

"What happened?" asked the third girl. "Stay off the walls, it's hot and dangerous!"

"They're afraid of me," Iria said. "I'm sorry, it's my aura."

"Why?" the third girl looked at Iria for a long moment. "You have six arms, that's not that scary."

Iria stepped closer and the girl did not budge. "You're not effected by my aura?" she asked. "How is that possible?"

"I'm not feeling any different since you got here, but my friends aren't having the same luck," said the girl. Iria backed away to help her friends get back to normal. The girl gathered her friends close. "Make way for us, I can get them downstairs!"

Iria returned to the first floor, where Griffen was waiting.

"We need to get out, this place is coming down!" Griffen yelled. "The people on the first floor were caught in the initial flame. Any luck upstairs?"

As Iria walked past Griffen, the three girls from upstairs came down, surrounded by a blue bubble that pushed aside the flames and allowed the three girls to exit, unscathed. Griffen exited last.

"What was that?" Griffen asked.

"My art," said the girl, pushing aside her messy short blonde hair from her eyes.

"You create force fields?" asked Iria.

"I do that, but I'm not great at it," the girl looked down at the ground, then put out her hand in Iria's direction. "I'm Merrill, by the way."

"I don't shake hands," said Iria.

"I'm Griffen, this is Iria," said Griffen. "You need to get out of here."

"We should keep her around," said Iria. "She isn't affected by my aura for some reason."

"Is that true?" Griffen asked Merrill.

"Seems that way," Merrill shrugged and said.

Furious that anyone survived his attack, Aerok roared again, his eyes lit red. When he went to blow fire, nothing happened. Dumbfounded, the beast stepped back and grabbed his throat with his right hand. He tried again, his eyes lighting up red once more, but nothing but a little smoke came out.

"Are you doing that?" Griffen looked at Merrill.

"Not intentionally, if I am," she responded. Merrill covered her body with her ragged clothing, as if she had something to be embarrassed about.

"Good idea to keep her around," Griffen said to Iria. "Looks like you lose, Aerok. The rest of my knights will be here soon from Dreadsmirk. You outsmarted us for the last time."

Aerok removed the bone blade from around his waist and smiled. He drew a line in the dirt in front of him.

"I've already won," Aerok said in the Dragonkin

language.

"Help Gerard," said Griffen. "Aerok is mine."

Griffen ran towards the dragon, removing his sword and clashing blades with the large beast. Iria led Merrill around the fight and joined Gerard and Faris in clearing out the Dragonkin in front of his home.

"Can you fight?" Iria asked.

"I've never fought anyone or anything before," Merrill said. "I'm just an orphan here. The people in the house I was in, were the ones taking care of me and the other girls."

Iria handed her one of the swords she got from the Wyndar shed. "Take one of my swords, just in case."

Merrill stayed back and held the sword awkwardly in her hands, hoping she wouldn't have to use it. Iria ran up beside Gerard and slashed at the Dragonkin he was fighting.

While those Dragonkin were being dealt with, Griffen and Aerok continued to exchange blows.

"I know you can't understand me, but this war is happening because of our actions on this day," Griffen began.

"You think I don't know that?" Aerok let out a rocky laugh. Griffen's face immediately displayed his shock, as Aerok's words spoke fluently in English. "Everything I've done today guarantees war between the humans and the dragons."

"Then our goals are similar," Griffen said, with a laugh of his own. "I wanted this war with your people just as bad."

"Then, win or lose, we both get what we want," Aerok answered. Despite his loud voice, the other knights were too far away to hear him.

"There isn't a choice," Griffen said, stepping back to keep some space between them. "No win or lose for you, I'm afraid. Just lose."

The light from the fire in the building behind Griffen created a large shadow beneath the dragon. The shadows rose off the ground and formed hands that grabbed the Dragonkin's tail and legs, and pinned it to the ground.

"There is a very powerful mage in Bawal who does my bidding. He can control shadows," Griffen walked around Aerok as he spoke. The dragon tried to grab him but he was just out of reach. "He's making this fight easy for me, as he did with Avernax when I slayed him."

Griffen completed a circle around the dragon, two more shadow hands tying up the dragon's arms, forcing him to drop his sword. Griffen walked right up to Aerok's face. "You think you're the one who started this war? No, you don't deserve that credit. This war is mine. I'd send you to warn Highborn, but you're dead."

Aerok went to speak, but Griffen drove his sword into the beast's throat. Aerok tried to grab Griffen, but the shadows prevented him. The blood in Aerok's throat began to gurgle as he collapsed to the ground.

"I will enjoy wiping out your kind," Griffen said, as he knelt down beside Aerok's limp body. As he stood up, he saw Wyglaf, Targen, Dawn and Grimoire entering the town from behind one of the houses.

"Grimoire, help me out with this fire problem?" he said and pointed at the house behind him with his thumb.

"Is that Aerok?" asked Wyglaf.

"Yes, he won't be terrorizing humans any longer," said Griffen.

"Heh, look at you," started Targen. "Here I was thinking you couldn't fight."

"Why would you think that?" asked Griffen, slightly offended.

"You just seem like the type of guy to hide in the shadows and let everyone else do your dirty work for you," Targen laughed. "I guess I have a new respect for you."

"Did he say anything in our language we could use to prevent this war from happening?" asked Dawn.

"Nothing I could understand," said Griffen. Grimoire finished putting out the fire behind them. "Gerard, Iria and Faris should be in the building over here."

When the other knights entered the building, they saw a similar scene that worried them. Blood on the floor and walls, the whole house was turned upside down in an obvious struggle. When the knights reached the last room in the back of the house, they found Gerard standing there with Faris, Iria and Merrill behind him. A pile of bodies lay in front of him.

"My mother..." Gerard began, his voice choking with emotion. "... and all of my siblings."

The rest of the knights entered the room. Wyglaf walked over and hugged Gerard, whose tears began to run down his face and onto Wyglaf's armor. Gerard patted Wyglaf's chest, before separating from him. Amily's body was draped on top of the pile. Gerard picked her up and cradled her in the same fashion that Dawn held her mother.

"This is all my fault," Gerard said. "I should have never left you."

"This isn't your fault, Gerard," said Griffen, stepping forward to join him and Wyglaf. "This is the fault of the Dragonkin, of Aerok Doomcaller and his pursuit to make this personal."

Griffen turned to face the rest of his Dragon Knights. "We can't continue to let these monsters inhabit the same Earth as us. We can't continue to let them roam unchecked, waiting in the wings to destroy our lands and take what is ours. Dawn's family, Gerard's family, the entire city of Davish...this is just the beginning. The Dragonkin got a taste of how easy it would be to burn our world to the ground and they aren't going to stop there."

"What do you suggest?" asked Grimoire.

"We return to Bawal for now. Regroup. Get Iria armed with proper weapons, analyze Merrill and find out what she can really do with her art. Train, not only with Wyglaf, but with each other. Learn from each other and get ready. Then we march on the Dragon Faux," he said, fire in his eyes. "They want to bring the fight to our homes, our families, then I say we do the same to them."

Chapter Ten

The next few days were pivotal for the knights. Dawn and Gerard took time to mourn, but also found comfort in getting outside and training. Dawn spent most of her time with Wyglaf, learning the ropes and expanding on the techniques that her father taught her. Faris spent most of his time with Grimoire and Gerard, to get a different aspect on things and master his speed. Targen didn't need much training, but Wyglaf convinced him to help train the others in hand-to-hand combat. Iria spent majority of her time with Griffen, her fascination with him grew stronger with each day, mainly for the fact that she considered him as the one who saved her. She continued to master her art along the way. She also spent a lot of time with Merrill, since she was the only one who could fully withstand her aura.

The necromancer of Bawal, Shadow, utilized a

sample of Merrill's blood to improve on his design for the bracelets that protected the knights from Iria's aura. He also ran tests on Iria to try to find the source of her power, but didn't have much luck in finding the cause of the aura itself. The most troublesome thing for all of the knights was the fact that Rappez, who had helped them early on in the start of this journey, was nowhere to be found when they returned to Bawal. Having been closest with him, this bothered Wyglaf the most and he sought answers. Those answers would come on the docks of Azuldra, where one of the first boats ever made on Khroma had just been finished being built. The aforementioned missing Bawal knight walked through the island closest to the water in Azuldra, Isone. On Isone, there had been built a great dock in anticipation for this day, when residents of Khroma would be able to sail the seas. Beside Rappez, walked Azadan.

"So, how does this work?" asked Azadan.

"The Millwake family has designed a device called the 'shore-liner' that calms the raging seas around Khroma and around the boat, therefore letting us sail," explained Rappez.

"Sounds interesting," Azadan responded. "I wonder what the islands around Khroma are like."

"Ready to be two of the first few to find out?" Rappez said with a smile, but his smile soon vanished at the sight of Wyglaf who was leaning against a random array of wooden boxes just in front of the boat. "Make your final preparations and then meet me here."

Azadan nodded and then walked past Wyglaf towards another set of wooden boxes, where Vallick was waiting for him. The two began talking, but Rappez zoned them out completely when Wyglaf broke the silence.

"I just want to know why," Wyglaf started. Rappez looked away from him, tongue pressing the inside of his cheek. "Why weren't you at the Wyndar mansion when we got there?"

"You want the honest truth?" Rappez said, leaning on a bannister across from Wyglaf that created a ramp to the ship. "I saw the dragons when I got there. They were already surrounding the mansion, and so I ran."

"You ran away?" Wyglaf asked harshly as he stood up straight. "Those dragons slaughtered Dawn's family!"

"They would have killed me too if I went in there!" Rappez stood up firmly as well. "I should have never become a knight of Bawal. I'm not willing to throw my life away so easily."

"With you, they had a fighting chance, Rappez. You left them there to die!" Wyglaf's loud voice drew the attention of the others around the dock.

"What do you want me to say, Wyglaf? That I'm a coward?" Rappez said and started to turn away, but Wyglaf grabbed his arm and turned him back to face him.

"I don't need you to say it. I already know you are," Wyglaf's words cut deep. "I thought I was starting to figure out the type of man you were, but I was wrong. I was completely wrong."

"The boat is leaving soon and I am in charge of making the preparations," Rappez said, turning away from Wyglaf once more.

"Go then. Go discover new places. I'll be here fighting for and protecting the one we already call home," Wyglaf said as he watched Rappez get onto the ship. "You will have to live with the death of Dawn's family on your conscience for the rest of your life!"

Azadan had gotten on the ship while they were talking, and the bridge of the ship pulled in shortly after Rappez got on. The boat began sailing away from Wyglaf ,who stared it down as it left.

"That was rough to watch," Vallick said as he walked up to Wyglaf. "You alright?"

"I'm fine," Wyglaf said. "Why didn't you go with them? Azadan is your mentor."

"Azadan and I both discovered something when we helped you fight those dragons," Vallick leaned on the bannister that Rappez was leaning on earlier. "Turns out I'm a better fighter now than both of us realized. He made it clear that there wasn't much more he could teach me and that I should go out and explore the world on my own."

"Exploring on your own is not nearly as fun as exploring with a group, take it from an old man who knows a thing or two," Wyglaf said with a smile.

"Is that an invite?" Vallick laughed.

"I think you would make a fine knight of Bawal," Wyglaf said. "I'm not just saying that, I saw the way you fight with that sword. Crimsonious, was it? Not sure how I feel about the name, but that's a fine blade."

"Yeah, Crimsonious makes me look better than I actually am," Vallick said. "Not sure I'm knight material though."

"But you certainly know how to handle a group of dragons," Wyglaf said. "We're forming a group to bring the fight to them. You don't need to make a decision right away, but if you want to join us, just come see me at Bawal. Even if you don't want to join, I might be able to teach you some things that Azadan left out. That is my original job, anyway."

"Thanks for the offer. I'll keep that in mind," Vallick said and offered his hand to Wyglaf, who accepted the gesture.

Epilogue

When Griffen next stepped foot in Diremoore, it was on behalf of Gerard. The first knight that joined his cause to put an end to the Dragonkin. Griffen kept his distance and watched Gerard from afar. Gerard stood in front of a small cemetery made beside the Pace manor, with a bouquet of flowers in his hand. His mother and his siblings tombstones served as a reminder of his choices and his mistakes.

"It was wrong of me to leave," Gerard began, tears building in his eyes. "You all deserved so much better. From me, from father...from this world. I left the burden on Amily and the one time I could have made a difference for her, I wasn't even there until it was too late. I didn't even get to say goodbye."

Gerard knelt down and placed the flowers on Amily's grave, which was positioned in the middle of their family. "This world was never fair to you. There was no reason you should have paid for my mistakes. I want you to know that the beasts that did this to you, will pay for what they've taken from us."

In the months that would follow, the newly formed Dragon Knights would spar and teach each other to become ten of the most efficient and feared fighters on Khroma. The tenth member eventually being Vallick, who chose to join the knights after discovering that Wyglaf was right; exploring the world by yourself can get boring after a while. Rappez and those who joined him on that journey to the islands outside Khroma, would not be heard from for years. Griffen's continued pleas to King Rebel for more knights to fight the dragons would continue to fall on deaf ears, as would his attempts to get the support of Sanctiveil, Azuldra and Ruebrum. In the end, it would remain the ten knights he recruited with Wyglaf and Gerard's help. Ten against thousands.

On the eve before the Dragon Knights would battle the Dragonkin on their home turf known as the Dragon Faux, Wyglaf stood in the middle of the Davish fields. The same place where the Wyndar mansion once stood. People continued to run the farms and grow fruit, but there was zero structure and most of the residents just grew fruit for their own individual profit. Wyglaf had his arms folded and on his back was a large shield made with a high dragon's skin. The stretched out face of the beast was in the center. Beside him stood Vallick, one hand on the handle of Crimsonious, now wearing the black armor of Bawal.

Not too far from the two Dragon Knights, was Dawn Wyndar. The plot that once had her home on it now only had the two graves of her parents. The months that passed visibly aged her, though she still looked young compared to most of the other knights. Her hair was now as long as her mother's and her face was more stern and mature. She held a long black spear in her right hand that diagonally crossed the back of her body, with the point facing the ground. She was a warrior now, as her father wanted her to be.

"I still don't know why things happened the way they did. I still don't understand why the dragons targeted our family," an occasional warm breeze would pass through Dawn's hair as she spoke. "I do know that the ones responsible still inhabit a large portion of this continent, and wish to do our people further harm. I now have the means to prevent that from happening and I will do so. In your names, as I have done everything up until this point, and will continue until the day I die."

Wyglaf walked up behind her. "Sorry to interrupt, Dawn. We have one last day to train before the big battle."

"Wyglaf," said Dawn as she turned her head slightly to look back at the veteran knight. The warm breeze had stopped. "I am ready."

About the Author

Joseph Angotti is the mastermind behind the world of Khroma and the ever-expanding universe of A Soldier's Crest, his debut novel. An avid fan of high fantasy, anime, and video games, he has combined elements from each to bring this fantasy to life. Joseph was born and raised in Queens, New York, where he draws the majority of his writing influence, and looks forward to branching out and sharing his stories with the rest of the world.

YOU HAVE JUST READ A BOOK PUBLISHED BY

THE POLYETHNIC PUBLISHING

THE POLYETHNIC PUBLISHING started out as a high school business project by then junior, Melissa Futrell. It wasn't until two years later when she launched the company after the success of The Polyethnic Taurus: Author Hop Tour in which she promoted many authors. Some of these are Michael Lackey, Michael Weekly, John I. Jones, and even New York Times #1 Bestselling Author, Karan Bajaj.

We are very honored that you have decided to buy this book and we cannot wait for you to see more of the titles we will be releasing. To learn more about us, our authors, and the books we will be publishing, visit our website at www.thepolyethnic.com.

Sincerely,
The Polyethnic Publishing

46091307R00083

Made in the USA
Middletown, DE
22 July 2017